Philips, Judson
Target for tragedy - Dodd, Mead, c1982.
188 p. - (A Red badge novel of suspense)

1. Detective and mystery stories. I. Title.

Target for Tragedy

Also by Judson Philips

Peter Styles Mysteries:

DEATH AS THE CURTAIN RISES
WHY MURDER?
A MURDER ARRANGED
FIVE ROADS TO DEATH
BACKLASH
WALK A CROOKED MILE
THE POWER KILLERS
THE LARKSPUR CONSPIRACY
THE VANISHING SENATOR
ESCAPE A KILLER
NIGHTMARE AT DAWN
HOT SUMMER KILLING
THURSDAY'S FOLLY
THE WINGS OF MADNESS
THE TWISTED PEOPLE
THE BLACK GLASS CITY
THE LAUGHTER TRAP

Target for Tragedy

A Red Badge Novel of Suspense

JUDSON PHILIPS

DODD, MEAD & COMPANY
NEW YORK

Printed in the United States of America

1 2 3 4 5 6 7 8 9 10

Library of Congress Cataloging in Publication Data

Philips, Judson Pentecost,
Target for tragedy.

(A Red badge novel of suspense)
I. Title.
PS3531.H442T3 813'.52 82-5088
ISBN 0-396-08079-0 AACR2

PART ONE

1

The house on the shore of Wynwood Lake in northwest Connecticut was called "the camp" by its owners. Its exterior was log cabin, but that ended any resemblance to a place for roughing it. Its own electric generator supplied power for heat, air conditioning, cooking, and refrigeration. If there was any gadget or system designed for luxury living missing, the man who was occupying the house as a tenant for the summer couldn't guess what it might have been.

It had problems for the tenant, however. There was a boathouse on the shore of the lake which contained an expensive power launch. The tenant had been left the keys to its twin-six engine. He was surrounded by the lake, by lovely woodland, and every adjunct for a relaxed, do-nothing vacation. The trouble was the tenant had come here to write a novel and he just couldn't get to it. The warm summer sun, the inviting lake with its areas for swimming, for fishing, for cruising in the power launch, were too much for a man who hadn't really relaxed for a good many years. Normally disciplined, the temptations were too great. His typewriter, set up in the pine-paneled living room, had remained untouched from dawn to dark for the first few days of the man's occupancy of the camp. After dark, after he had made himself a supper exactly to his taste, preceded by two dry martinis made exactly the way he liked them, he sat at the machine, staring at a blank sheet of paper, trying to get started on something he'd thought was carefully planned.

The thing that had at first seemed so ideal to the tenant of the camp was its complete privacy. From the deck outside the living room windows you had a marvelous view of the lake, but no sign of a house anywhere. The town road was four or five hundred yards up through the woods above the camp, so there was no traffic. No one would ever interfere with the work process by chance. You would have to know where the camp was to find it. You wouldn't be likely to stumble on it by accident. And yet, on the third night of "a summer for writing," the tenant's privacy was invaded and in a rather extraordinary fashion.

The tenant, a man in his thirties, slender, wiry, with expensively trimmed dark hair and very bright blue eyes, had just ripped a sheet of paper out of his typewriter, crumpled it into a ball, and tossed it away with a gesture of disgust, when he heard a woman's voice, some distance from the house, raised in what might have been a squeal of delight. Summertime, a full moon, a time for romantic nonsense, the tenant thought.

Then the voice was closer, this time articulating, "Bob! Please! *Please!*"

"Oh, for God's sake," the tenant thought.

Then someone was running across the wooden deck outside the windows, pounding now, violently, on the front door. The man at the typewriter started to rise when the door burst open—it wasn't locked—and a young woman appeared to be literally catapulted into the room. She was halfway across the room toward the man when she stopped in her tracks, brown eyes wide with what he saw was terror.

"Bob?" she said in a strangled voice.

"Bob isn't here," the man said.

"Where?"

The man's smile was friendly, reassuring. "My best guess would be Athens, Greece," he said. The girl moved a step or two to grab the back of a chair, as if she needed to hold herself up. "My name is Peter Styles," the man said. "Bob and Betty have let me have this place for the summer while they make the grand tour of Europe."

"I—I'm so sorry—to barge in like this," the girl said. "I saw the lights in the windows—" She looked as if her legs were going to give out entirely.

"Please do sit down," Peter Styles said. "I have some fresh coffee over there in the machine on the sideboard. Slug of booze to go with it?"

The girl moved around the chair and sat down. She raised unsteady hands to cover her face. Peter Styles crossed the room to the front door that still stood open. He listened for a moment and heard nothing except the call of a night bird. He closed the door and came back into the room. He stood by the girl whose whole body was trembling, waiting for her to speak. Then he moved over to the sideboard, poured coffee into a china mug and some brandy into a measuring glass and brought them back to the table beside the girl's chair.

"What frightened you?" he asked.

The girl lowered her hands and her wide brown eyes looked at Peter Styles, uncertain whether he was friend or foe. His name should have been enough to reassure her. In this part of the world he was recognized as the star investigative reporter for *Newsview* magazine. He had gained considerable fame in the free world as a crusader against senseless violence, a disease of the times. His name had apparently meant nothing to the girl.

"You're good friends with Bob and Betty Jordan?" he asked.

She nodded.

"But you didn't know they'd gone away for four months?"

Just that blank, uncertain look. "I am Judith Larsen," she said, as though that explained everything.

"Look, Judith," he said, "I'm not up on local personalities. First, is there some kind of trouble out there? Does someone out there need help?"

"I needed help!" the girl said. "I saw the lights. I knew Bob and Betty would—would believe me and help!"

"Tell me what it is and I'll help," Peter Styles said.

The girl, her arms clasped around her midsection, rocked

back and forth in the chair. "The same man," she said. "This time he—he fired a shot at me when I ran. There was no place to go but here!"

"Someone shot at you?"

"The same man," she said. "The same ski mask."

"Ski mask! For God's sake, child, this is June!"

"Everybody in the world knows my story!" she cried out.

"With at least one exception," Peter said.

"Do you have a car, Mr. Stein?"

"It's Styles," he said. "Try Peter."

"Would you consider driving me back to the village?"

"Of course," Peter said. "But about this character who took a shot at you?"

"I don't think he'll try anything again unless I'm alone," the girl said.

Peter reached for his jacket, which was hung over the chair by his typewriter, and slipped into it. "If you don't want to talk you don't have to," he said.

"Anybody in Wynwood can tell you my story—Peter," she said. Her smile was bitter. "I'm a celebrity."

"A celebrity who runs screaming through the woods, chased by a man in a ski mask who takes potshots at her?"

The girl just twisted from side to side like someone in pain.

In a tall crockery jar just to the right of the front door the Jordans kept an umbrella and several walking sticks. Peter selected a sturdy-looking blackthorn with a large round knob for a handle.

"Just in case," Peter said.

As they stepped out onto the deck Peter reached back inside and switched off the lights. The moon, nearly full, bathed the camp, the surrounding woods, and the lake in something like silvery daylight. Peter and the girl walked around the deck to the rear of the house where Peter's car, a compact little Toyota, was parked under a lean-to. Peter, scanning the woods for sight of someone, stood by as the girl got into the passenger seat. Then he walked around the car, got in himself, started the motor and switched on the headlights.

"Where to, Miss Judith Larsen?" he asked, smiling at her.

Her lips moved as though they were stiff. "I live with my mother and stepfather," she said. "He runs Maxi-Service and the house is back of the business yard."

"I'm just three days here," Peter said. "I'm afraid I don't know Wynwood yet. What is Maxi-Service?"

"My stepfather takes care of all the big estates," she said. "He has a crew of men who mow lawns, trim hedges, do gardening—any outside work for the big houses in town. Plow snow out of your driveway in wintertime. The yard where he stores his trucks and equipment is just off the village green. It's only about a mile from your entrance."

Peter glanced at his wristwatch. It was just after ten o'clock. "There'll be someone there?" he asked.

She nodded. That was all. Peter had seen people in shock before in his life, and Judith Larsen was very close to it. Getting her to her own people was all he knew to do for her.

Five or six minutes later they were driving along Wynwood's beautiful village green. When Bob and Betty Jordan had offered Peter the camp for the summer, they'd told him that Wynwood might just be "the richest town in the world."

"Rich and socially prominent people retired, built homes there at the turn of the century," Bob Jordan told Peter. "Their children and grandchildren have retired to the same estates. There are two populations, the very rich and the people who serve them—butcher, baker, candlestick maker! Nothing happens there except luxury, tranquility, in elegantly kept country estates. Strangers, even famous ones, are not encouraged, so you won't be lionized. It should be an ideal place for you to hole in and get your book started."

Nothing happens, Peter thought, except a man in a ski mask takes shots at a frightened girl in the moonlight!

"The turnoff is just ahead to the left, Mr. Styles," Judith said.

"Peter," he said.

"Peter."

About a quarter of a mile after the left turn Peter saw a cluster of barns and sheds separated from the road by a wide gravel yard. At an entrance was a sign proclaiming "MAXI-SERVICE."

"You turn in here," the girl said. "The house is just up a rise behind the barns. And—and I'm very, very grateful."

"I haven't done anything but give you a lift," Peter said.

"I hope it doesn't cost you," Judith said, her voice husky. "It isn't healthy to get involved with me."

The house, up behind the barns and sheds, was a beautiful old Colonial that looked as if it had been rooted in the earth forever. Warm lights glowed in both the downstairs and upstairs windows. The family who lived here was obviously still up and about.

As the Toyota negotiated the circular driveway and its headlights swept across the face of the house, the front door opened and a large, powerfully built man came out onto the front steps. Peter felt Judith's fingers close tightly on his arm.

"My stepfather," she said. Peter had stopped the car at the foot of the path leading up to the front door. Judith turned her head to look at him. "Again—thanks so very much."

Peter smiled at her. "Come again, anytime," he said.

She got out of the car and ran up the path. To Peter's surprise she went straight past her stepfather without speaking, nor did the man appear to make any effort to speak to her or stop her. Instead, he raised an arm in a gesture to Peter that asked him to wait.

The man who came down the path was wearing corduroy slacks and a red-and-blue plaid sports shirt, open at the throat. The sleeves of the shirt were rolled up and the forearms were thick and muscular. His face and those forearms were tanned a mahogany brown. He came around the car to Peter's side.

"I'm George Wilson, Judith's stepfather," he said.

"I'm Peter Styles," Peter said.

"Ah, yes. You've rented the Jordans' camp for the summer?"

Something about the harsh voice, the narrowed brown eyes, rubbed Peter the wrong way. "You keep track, Mr. Wilson?"

"I do some outside work for the Jordans," Wilson said. "Keep the brush cut and the trees trimmed in their woodland plot. They told me, before they took off, they were renting their place to Peter Styles, the *Newsview* writer. May I ask how you happened to make contact with Judith?"

"You may ask and you should know," Peter said. "I was working in the camp when I heard someone running along the deck, and then Judith burst into the house. She expected to find the Jordans. Unlike you, she evidently didn't know I'd rented the place. She told me a man, wearing a ski mask, had frightened her in the woods and taken a shot at her when she ran. She came to the camp because she thought she'd find friends."

"Oh, Lord!" Wilson said. He didn't sound distressed, more like a man who's hearing an old and boring story.

"She said something strange to me," Peter said. " 'The same man—the same ski mask.' Then she said, 'Everybody in the world knows my story.' Unfortunately, I don't. She wouldn't tell me any more, but she was scared out of her wits so I drove her home."

Wilson nodded as though he was hearing a familiar tune.

"I noticed she didn't stop to tell you what had happened," Peter said.

Wilson's big chest expanded as he took a deep breath and

let it out in something like a sigh. "I have to tell you, Mr. Styles, that Judith is a very sick girl. Almost certainly what she told you was pure imagination."

"But she'd had an encounter at some other time with a man in a ski mask?"

"A nightmare, I'm afraid, that she builds on and repeats. Look, Mr. Styles, Judith is sick. She's under medical care. She imagines strange things that never really happen. I appreciate very much your bringing her home. But it's our problem and we'll deal with it."

Peter had the uncomfortable feeling that if he accepted what Wilson was telling him and took off, he'd be leaving Judith in the hands of the enemy.

"Her mother is at home? Is that who she's run to?" he asked.

Wilson nodded. "Please, Mr. Styles, this is a private difficulty. Accept our gratitude and let us handle it."

Peter looked at the house. He had the feeling he might see Judith at one of the windows, gesturing to him. There was nothing. He looked back at Wilson. "Tell Judith if she wants to visit the camp again she's welcome."

"I'll tell her, Mr. Styles."

Almost reluctantly, Peter drove down the incline into the Maxi-Service yard and out onto the main road. He had a highly developed instinct for a story, and something about George Wilson's write-off of his stepdaughter's tale didn't sit with him. He recalled seeing at the north end of town the red brick state police barracks, and he headed in that direction. Arriving there, he asked for whoever was in charge and was taken into a small office where an officer wearing sergeant's stripes was holding down a desk. A desk sign told Peter this was Sergeant Quinlan.

"My name is Peter Styles," he said.

"Let's see, you've rented the Jordans' place for the

summer," Quinlan said. "How can I help you, Mr. Styles?"

As Peter told the sergeant about Judith Larsen's appearance at the camp and her story of a man in a ski mask—"the same man in the same ski mask"—Quinlan's stiff, official mask seemed to relax. Once more Peter got the impression of someone listening to an old, familiar story.

"George Wilson tells me his stepdaughter is ill," Peter said, "but if some creep is wandering around my place taking shots at people, I'd like the area checked out."

"You hear any shots, Mr. Styles?"

"No, but I was concentrating on what I was trying to do—which is to get a book started. If there was a shot I might not have paid any attention—kids fooling around in the woods on a summer night."

The sergeant leaned forward, picked up the receiver on his desk phone, and dialed a number. "Hello—Doc?—Mike Quinlan here." He laughed. "No, no accident, no dead body for you. But are you up and around or have you gone to bed? Well, there's a man named Peter Styles here. Yes, he writes for *Newsview*, living in the Jordan place. He's had an encounter with Judith Larsen. . . . Yeah, poor kid. A man in a ski mask taking shots at her, she says. . . . Yes. . . . I don't think it's proper for me to go into this with Mr. Styles, but I thought you might be willing to put a few cards on the table for him. . . . Well, naturally he's uneasy if there's someone hanging around his place taking shots at people. . . . Thanks, Doc. He'll be along in a few minutes." Quinlan put down the phone and shoved it aside. "Dr. Jonathan Smalley, he's our town man," he said. "In particular he's Judith's doctor and he can straighten you out, I think. Head back into town and you'll pass the post office on your left. Doc Smalley's is the second house past it; his name's on a sign on the front gatepost.

"What about checking out my place?" Peter asked.

"I have to tell you, Mr. Styles, I don't think what Judith told you ever really happened. We've been there before. But I have a personal reason for wanting to protect her from another big stink. Let Doc Smalley put you straight."

It wasn't what you would think of as a routine police response to a request for help. Peter reminded himself that this was a small town. Here the state police would know everyone, be prepared to handle things in the light of that knowledge. Quinlan was sending him for nonofficial answers to questions that were bothering him. To prevent him from starting "another big stink"?

"You have any reason, after you talk to Doc Smalley, to think there are any prowlers around your place, Mr. Styles, give me a call and I'll have someone there in five minutes."

"You can count on it," Peter said. He paused in the office door. "I'll be in to say thank you, Sergeant, if I find you're not giving me some kind of runaround."

Quinlan grinned at him. "Like most reporters, you don't trust the cops, right?"

"Only time lets you trust anyone in this world, Sergeant."

It was going on eleven o'clock when Peter stopped his car outside Dr. Smalley's house. It was brightly lighted inside and there were porch lights. Other houses on the green were dark, indicating that Wynwood went to bed at a reasonably early hour. As he walked up the path the front door to the house was opened and a tall, rather stooped, gray-haired man came out on the porch to greet him. The doctor must be in his late sixties, early seventies, Peter thought. Time had left a pleasant, kindly face, deeply lined. Blue eyes were bright, questioning, perceptive. This was a man who looked for clues to character in a stranger.

"Mr. Styles?" A quiet, well-modulated voice.

"Thank you for seeing me, Dr. Smalley," Peter said.

"Come in," the doctor said, holding open the door for his guest.

"This isn't a very civilized hour to be paying a call on a stranger," Peter said. He looked back out at the green. "Most of the village seems to have turned in."

"I watch the lights go out every night," Dr. Smalley said. "My trade has made me a fitful sleeper. Night is the time when most people really need my help. The age when doctors made house calls is pretty much a thing of the past, but I still respond when people ask for help. Can't get out of the habit. And I've known most of the people in Wynwood all of my life. They're my friends."

The doctor's living room was simple, undistinguished, but it had a lived-in, comfortable look.

"My housekeeper leaves me a coffeepot going round the clock," Dr. Smalley said. " 'To what do you attribute your good health in your old age, Doctor?' My answer is, 'Fifteen cups of coffee and three packs of cigarettes a day.' Hard to make my patients behave with that example. Can I tempt you, Mr. Styles?"

"I'm as bad as you are about coffee," Peter said.

The doctor left the room for a moment. Peter noticed a rather good winter landscape hanging over the stone fireplace. Smalley might not be a collector, but what he had was rather special. There were artists and writers in the town, Bob Jordan had said. Evidently a skillful one was the doctor's friend.

The doctor came back with two crockery mugs of coffee. "Sugar or cream or both?" he asked. "I'm a straight man myself."

"I, too," Peter said. He sat down in a comfortable chair the doctor indicated.

"Mike Quinlan, who, by the way, is a first-rate young officer, tells me you've had an encounter with Judith Larsen and one of her fantasies."

"If it was a fantasy," Peter said. The coffee was hot, excellent.

"That poor child has been a target for tragedy all of her life," the doctor said.

2

The doctor sat down facing Peter, his long legs stretched out in front of him. He took a cigarette out of his pocket and lit it with a cheap lighter. Peter saw that his long, tapering fingers were stained yellow with nicotine.

"Bother you?" the doctor asked. He smiled. "I never ask till I've got one going."

"You're the doctor," Peter said. "About Judith?"

The doctor exhaled a cloud of smoke. "She was born here in Wynwood," he said. "So were her parents, Kurt and Rose Larsen. Kurt was a fine man, not well educated but decent and good. Judith was an only child, and she idolized her father. When she was about twelve years old—that would be eight years ago—Kurt was killed. He worked for George Wilson, who owns and runs Maxi-Service. He was driving a truckload of machinery to a job somewhere. We assumed the truck's brakes gave out as he was going down Wynwood Mountain. Kurt lost control and the truck went off the road and somersaulted down into a deep gorge. It was smashed to pieces, caught fire, and it—and Kurt—were burned to ashes. Little Judith went into a kind of hysterical shock. Kurt meant everything to her. The whole town was grieved, because Kurt was a good man."

"And she's stayed in shock for eight years?" Peter asked.

"That, Mr. Styles, was only just the beginning," the doctor said. He reached for the ashtray on the table beside his chair and missed it. The debris on the table top suggested he often missed. "She did pretty well for a kid who had lost the center, the core, of her world. She went on to high school, was a good student, came out of the period of gloom with flags flying. I admired her because I knew how rough it had been for her. But, as I say, that was just the beginning.

"When Judith was a junior in high school her mother told her that she was going to marry George Wilson, who had been her father's boss.

"I don't think Judith had thought that anyone could ever take Kurt's place, certainly not with her, and I think she felt that Rose, her mother, was somehow betraying Kurt. But the townspeople were pleased. Rose and George, each alone, needed each other. George is very well off and that meant there'd be no problems about Judith going on to college. I think George tried hard with Judith, and while she accepted him as her mother's husband, she just couldn't let him be a father to her. I think it's hurt him, particularly after what happened to Rose."

"I understood she was there at the house, living there," Peter said.

"*Living* is a word that can have shades of meaning," Dr. Smalley said. "Rose is alive—in a medical sense."

"Medical sense?"

"Three years ago, when Judith was entering her senior year in high school, the Fates took another whack at that kid," Smalley said. "One evening George was working on his accounts in the dining room of their house. Judith was upstairs in her room, doing her homework. They both heard a scream and a terrible thudding sound. There is a freezer in the basement of the house where they store meats, herbs, other things. Rose, who'd been working in the kitchen, had apparently started down to get something from that freezer. She tripped and plunged down a steep flight of stairs to the concrete floor in the basement." The doctor shook his head. "She was rushed to the hospital in Winston. I rode in the ambulance with her—head smashed in, broken leg, broken arm, internal injuries. She had the best care, surgical and otherwise, that money could provide."

"And?"

The doctor looked steadily at Peter. "She's a vegetable, Mr. Styles. No contact with anyone, unable to feed herself, keep herself clean. A nothing!"

"God!" Peter said.

"I told you Judith is a target for tragedy," the doctor said. "That's not the end of it, Mr. Styles. George Wilson did everything humanly possible for Rose. Eventually he brought her home, just to sit and stare into space. He hired a practical nurse who lives there round the clock. Judith came to me, desperate. Was there any chance her mother might someday look at her and recognize her? If there wasn't she had to get away. She didn't belong in George Wilson's house. I had to tell her that maybe, sometime later, Nature might work a miracle. And so Judith stayed, and has stayed ever since. But she almost got away. She almost made it, but once again tragedy was waiting for her."

"What else could happen?"

"The man she came to love was murdered," Dr. Smalley said.

Peter sat very still, waiting for him to go on. He had forgotten his coffee and it had grown cold in the crockery mug.

"Judith was twenty this last fall," Dr. Smalley said. "After the fact, and from talking to her friends, she wasn't typical of most girls in their high school years. Went to school dances, and parties, but never seemed to have any one special guy at any time—until Dick Robbins came along.

Dick was one of the prize 'locals.' We call the native people locals to differentiate them from I suppose you'd say 'the landed gentry.' Dick Robbins, by the way, is the reason why you're here, Mr. Styles. Dick and Mike Quinlan grew up together, went to high school together, and to college. Played on the same football and baseball teams, star athletes. They took the training and became state troopers together. A sort of Damon and Pythias combination. Prize kids, we thought of them as they grew up, and prize young men as they became a part of our security. Mike Quinlan sent you here because Dick Robbins meant so very much to him."

"I'm letting you lead the way, Doctor," Peter said.

"I don't know for certain how Dick Robbins and Judith got together," the doctor said. "He was, I think, about five years older than she, so it couldn't have been at school. In any case, they did get together and it was real, honest-to-goodness love at first sight. They announced their engagement. Locally, everyone was pleased. Judith deserved some happiness, and everyone thought she'd make a fine wife for Dick. He bought a piece of property where they planned to build a house. It's just across the road that runs above the house where you're staying. Dick got a leave of absence. They were to be married, in the home of the local minister, the first day of that leave and take off on their honeymoon. Then, the last night that Dick was on patrol duty, it happened."

"You said 'murder'?"

"It was a car chase," the doctor said, nodding slowly. "Dick Robbins reported in on his patrol-car radio that he'd seen a car that aroused his suspicion coming out of one of the big estates. The owners were away and the troopers had been alerted to keep an eye on things. When Dick signaled this car to stop for questioning it took off out of town at high speed. Dick gave chase and finally forced the other car over to the side of the road. He got out of his patrol car and went over to talk to them—that's what the troopers figured out from evidence at the scene—and he was shot dead. Bullets in the head, chest. Quick, instant, final."

"Killers got away?"

"Yes. Dick Robbins had reported the car's license number to the barracks during the chase. A Connecticut car, but it developed that the plate had been stolen off a Connecticut car. No way to trace the car on which the stolen plate had been placed. I believe Dick had said it was a black Lincoln-Mercury. Dead end."

"Just the night before the wedding day," Peter said. "How long ago was this, Doctor?"

"About six months. You can imagine the state Judith was in. It was, I'm afraid, one too many for her. Dick had represented an escape from tragedy for her, and instead he just compounded it."

"But that doesn't account for tonight—what you and Sergeant Quinlan seem to think was some kind of fantasy?"

"Judith didn't have any close friends to turn to at that terrible time," the doctor said. "Mike Quinlan was to have been the best man at the wedding and his young wife, Nora, Judith's maid of honor. But they were Dick Robbins's friends, not Judith's. They did what they could for her. Her mother was no use to her, and she and George Wilson had never really hit it off. It was a private torture time for her, and she took it very hard."

"Not to be blamed for that," Peter said.

"About six weeks ago, a lovely spring evening, she went for a walk. It was a habit she'd developed after Dick's death, walking out alone in the evening. It seems she always walked out to the little piece of property in the woods that Dick had bought, where their dream house was to have been built. Maybe she felt closer to him there, to the times they'd spent there together. On this particular night, actually a little after midnight, Mike Quinlan was driving a regular road patrol."

"That's Sergeant Quinlan?"

The doctor nodded. "Quinlan's route took him along the road that runs just above your camp, bordering the property Dick had bought. Suddenly someone came out of the woods beside the road, waving some kind of a tree branch at him. The person had to know he was a trooper—car with red and blue lights on the roof. Quinlan stopped, got out, gun at the ready. What he found was Judith, hysterical, covering herself with that tree branch." The doctor raised his head to look at Peter. "She was stark naked!"

"Come again!" Peter said.

"Naked as the day she was born. Incoherent story. She'd been sitting up on Dick's property when a man, wearing a ski mask, had attacked her, beaten her, fondled her, raped her. He had left her, half unconscious. When she came to, she couldn't find her clothes anywhere. She broke off a couple of small leafy branches from a tree to cover herself and went down to the road to try to flag someone for help."

"Not a fantasy," Peter said, realizing his voice wasn't quite steady.

The doctor lit himself a fresh cigarette. His eyes were narrowed against the smoke. "Mike covered her with a canvas tarpaulin the troopers carry in their cars—to cover bodies in case they find themselves dealing with a fatal automobile accident. He brought her straight here to my office. Judith was in a pitiable state of hysteria. We didn't get too clear a story from her until later. I sedated her, examined her. There were multiple bruises and scratches, as though she might have been dragged through brush. I sent for an ambulance and had her taken to the hospital in Winston. There the doctors made a discovery." The doctor shook his head from side to side. "Dick Robbins had had something rather special waiting for him. Special in this day and age. He would have found himself with a twenty-year-old bride who was a virgin."

"But if she had just been raped—?"

"Whatever this man in the ski mask had done to her he had not, to use the medical phrase, 'penetrated' her."

"Then she wasn't raped?"

The doctor flicked the ash from his cigarette, ignoring the ashtray altogether. "Legally, yes," he said. "In the sense we usually think of it, no. But the point is, did anything happen to her at all?"

"I don't understand," Peter said.

"The psychiatrist at the hospital doubts it," Dr. Smalley said. "Judith was a girl driven over the brink by a succession of disasters. Dr. Kreuger thinks the whole thing may have been some sort of paranoid fantasy."

"I still don't understand," Peter said. "You say there were bruises, scratches—as though she'd been dragged through the brush."

"Self-inflicted, Kreuger thinks. She could have torn off her own clothes, thrown herself down on the rocks and into the bushes in some kind of demented state."

"They found her clothes."

"No."

"She's supposed to have taken her evening walk naked?"

"There's a rapid stream running down to the lake up there. You probably know it. It doesn't pass too far from your camp. She could have tossed her clothes into the stream and they would be out in the lake, long gone."

"But why disbelieve her in the first place? Just because she'd been the victim of tragedy? I've had a pretty tough time in my life, but that doesn't make me a mental case," Peter said.

"Her story was inconsistent."

"And no 'penetration'?"

"Why would a rapist go as far as he did and not the whole way?" Dr. Smalley asked.

"Maybe they should find him and ask him," Peter said.

"They've tried. There's simply nothing to lead them anywhere."

Peter stood up. He found himself suddenly angry. "So they won't believe her story tonight? Is that why I'm here, Doctor?"

"I guess, so," the doctor said. "So you'll understand why they won't believe it. Mike Quinlan, who sent you here, is her friend, you know."

"The whole town knows her story and believes she's some kind of crazy trying to tell the world that she's still wanted by some maniac? Is that what she meant when she told me she was a 'celebrity'?"

"I'm afraid so," the doctor said. "It's a great something to chew on at the cocktail hour, you know."

"And you, Doctor? You think it's all fantasy?"

The old doctor stretched his long legs and stood up to face Peter. "I wish I could answer that with any real conviction either way, Mr. Styles. The troopers and Dr. Kreuger think she's a very sick, disturbed girl. I wish I could prove she was telling the truth, because I like her and have a very real sympathy for her and what she's been through."

"But you really go with the cops and your shrink friend?"

"Show me how to go some other way," the doctor said.

"Maybe I will," Peter said. "Something about this just doesn't ring true, Dr. Smalley."

"Judith's story or mine?" Dr. Smalley asked.

It was nearly midnight when Peter drove back into the yard at the state trooper barracks. Sergeant Quinlan was straightening out his desk, just about to go off duty, when Peter walked into the office.

"I take it Doc Smalley put you wise, Mr. Styles."

"He told me why you sent me to him," Peter said. "I'd like to talk. Here? Or at my place? I'll buy you a drink."

Quinlan hesitated. "I live just about a mile away," he said. "I'll buy *you* a drink. It might be useful if my wife sat in on the conversation. She's Judith's friend."

"I'm glad to hear she has one," Peter said.

The Quinlans lived in a pleasant cottage on a high rise of ground that looked down on the village green. Nora Quinlan was an attractive girl with dark red hair and very bright eyes that suggested humor. She was obviously a little embarrassed at being found wearing a dressing gown and barefooted by a stranger, but she didn't make any apologies or excuses.

"You're the *Newsview* reporter, aren't you, Mr. Styles?" she asked. And when he admitted he was, "I don't always agree with what you say, Mr. Styles, but I love the way you say it."

"Right now I think Mr. Styles thinks we're throwing him a curve," Quinlan said. "Can you rustle up some cheese and crackers and a drink, hon?"

"It'll have to be bourbon or gin, Mr. Styles," Nora said.

"First I'd like to talk," Peter said. "Maybe afterward."

"I better bring you up-to-date, hon," Quinlan said to his wife. "Mr. Styles had a run-in with Judith. That man in the ski mask has turned up again."

"Oh, wow!" Nora Quinlan said.

"Would you tell it to Nora, Mr. Styles?" Quinlan asked.

The girl listened intently as Peter told of a cry in the woods, the running footsteps on the camp's deck, and Judith bursting into the room. He told of driving her home and getting nothing really factual from her, of George Wilson's brushoff, and of his eventual meeting with Dr. Smalley at Quinlan's suggestion.

"Poor kid," Nora said. "She's really had it!"

"Your husband and Dr. Smalley seem to think that the

rape story and what Judith says happened tonight are sick dream-ups," Peter said.

"It's like a fighter who gets knocked down a couple of times in the early rounds," Quinlan said, "and recovers fine. Then he gets a third knockdown later and his knees buckle and he doesn't know where his corner is."

"And then dreams up other knockdowns that never happened?"

"Something like that," Quinlan said.

"The bruises and scratches on her body?" Peter asked.

"And her mouth was swollen and hurt," Nora said.

"She claimed the man in the ski mask hit her?"

Nora shook her head. "She says the man ripped off her clothes, wrestled her to the ground, tried to kiss her—brutally. Fondled her breasts, rolled her around. She says she broke away and ran and he caught up with her, tackled her and brought her down in a clump of brambles."

"And never went the whole way sexually?"

"That's what she says."

"And the hospital examination proved it," Quinlan said.

"It's hard for me to accept the picture," Peter said. "This girl goes out to the property where she and her dead lover planned to build a house. Suddenly she goes into some kind of deranged frenzy, tears off her clothes, throws them in a running stream, hurls herself on the rocky ground and into a clump of bramble bushes, bruises her own mouth, and then runs out into the road, naked, to flag down a car."

"That's Dr. Kreuger's diagnosis," Quinlan said.

"What kind of a character is this Dr. Kreuger?" Peter asked.

"I work for him," Nora said very quietly. "That is to say, I work in the psychiatric clinic at the hospital where he's the head doctor."

"As a human being he's a horse's ass!" Quinlan said, his voice angry. "As a doctor he rates at the top."

Nora lowered her eyes. "Dr. Kreuger is a womanizer,"

she said. "I'm one of dozens of women he's made a pass at. Mike doesn't like him."

"But you stay on the job?"

"Because I made it clear to the sonofabitch that I'd break his neck if he ever looked at Nora again," Quinlan said.

"I majored in psychology in college," Nora said. "I trained to be a psychiatric nurse. Dr. Kreuger runs the best clinic of its kind in this part of the world. There's the money in this community to give him everything he needs. As long as the doctor understands that I'm out of bounds I'd be crazy not to work at what I know is the best place there is."

"So, I'm talking to a qualified expert in the field when I talk to you," Peter said. "You are Judith's friend. You knew her before all this happened. Do you agree with Kreuger's diagnosis?"

"When you say 'all this,' Mr. Styles—I didn't know Judith as a young girl, when her father died and her mother had that terrible fall. I'm not from Wynwood myself. Mike and I met in college and we were married after he joined the state police. I knew Dick Robbins in college. He was Mike's best friend. But I didn't know Judith till she became engaged to Dick. He brought her here, introduced her to us, only about a year ago. A few months later he was dead."

"Dick was like a brother to me," Mike Quinlan said. "Judith was his girl, and after he was killed, we stood by her for his sake. Nora wasn't close at all till after Dick was gone."

"And then she was disturbed, hysterical," Peter said. "So, do you agree with Dr. Kreuger?"

Nora hesitated just long enough to suggest doubt. "He could be right," she said.

"There's the police angle," Mike Quinlan said. "Our investigation was more than ordinarily thorough, Mr.

Styles. We never got a clue to Dick Robbins's killer, and when this rape thing happened we thought there might be some connection. Judith was Dick's girl. I was in on it. There wasn't a trace of anyone else up there in the woods where the rape is supposed to have happened."

"Footprints?" Peter asked.

"Dry, leafy ground," Quinlan said. "Doesn't take prints. There was evidence in the brush that something had happened there—branches broken off. If there was a man involved you'd hope to find a piece of torn cloth, anything that might prove his existence. There were no signs of any tire tracks where a car might have been parked near Dick's property."

"It's still his property?" Peter asked.

"He left it to Judith," Quinlan said.

"There's another slant to it, Mr. Styles," Nora said. "Judith's history didn't involve men. There was no rejected suitor, no lover from another time. Dick was apparently the first man she was ever close to. There wasn't a single thing in the past that suggested some kind of reprisal."

"So she's declared mentally deranged," Peter said. "Isn't it possible there's some man around who's off his trolley? Some geek just passing through town?"

"Why would a girl who had been so brutally attacked go back to the same place again, after dark, at night?" Nora asked.

"Because she didn't dream it would happen again," Peter said. "Probably thought the man who'd attacked her was on the other side of the earth by now. It was her place, where she'd dreamed her romantic dreams. Why not go back? The good things the place represented to her far outweighed that one ghastly night."

Nora looked at him steadily. "Can I ask you a question, Mr. Styles."

"Of course."

"You never met Judith or heard her story until tonight?"

"True."

"Why are you so ready to disbelieve the police who handled her case and the doctors who cared for her?" Nora asked.

Peter was silent for a moment. "No reason that will make the slightest sense to you," he said finally. "As a reporter I've been involved with violence for quite a few years, not just crimes you read about in the papers, but personally! I'll tell you about it sometime. The result is a highly developed instinct about violent crime. Hunches. Experience has made me trust those hunches. I've seen people in shock, in hysterics. I've had to make guesses about them a hundred times. Better than ninety percent of those guesses have been right. I have a hunch that what Judith told me tonight actually happened. I don't know about the rape thing, but tonight I think she was telling the truth. Someone approached her, took a shot at her when she ran."

"Someone wearing a ski mask?" Quinlan asked.

"Maybe, maybe not," Peter said. "In the darkness, in the woods, she may have imagined the mask."

"If there ever was anyone wearing a mask! I tell you, Mr. Styles, the whole thing is a sick invention."

"And don't think we haven't the deepest sympathy for Judith," Nora Quinlan said. "If she could only be persuaded to follow Dr. Kreuger's advice."

"Which is?"

"To get out of town, somewhere completely away from Wynwood, away from all the tragic associations it has for her. But she won't."

"Because of her mother?"

Nora nodded.

"She was going to be married."

"And live less than a mile away," Nora Quinlan said. "Always on call, always at the ready in case her mother ever shows a sign of life." She smiled at Peter. "Bourbon and soda, or water?" she asked.

"How did you know it wasn't going to be gin?" Peter asked.

Her smile widened. "Hunch," she said. "And better than ninety percent of my hunches pay off."

Nora Quinlan had skillfully broken the tension that was growing between Peter and her husband. Peter realized that his reliance on hunches must be enormously irritating to Mike Quinlan, who had investigated the original "rape" case and found nothing whatever to substantiate it. Quinlan had something more than a stiff-necked policeman's attitude toward the case. He had a genuine sympathy for Judith Larsen or he wouldn't have sent Peter to Dr. Smalley. But the combination of no evidence to support Judith's story of being stripped naked and assaulted and Dr. Kreuger's diagnosis of her mental condition left him with no way to accept the hunches of a complete stranger. Quinlan would, Peter thought, have liked to prove Dr. Kreuger wrong. He hated his wife's boss, but he had to believe in Kreuger's medical competence.

Drinks and a Vermont cheddar cheese and crackers led to casual talk, mostly about the town of Wynwood.

"Kind of a feudal society," Quinlan said. "The big landowners, the feudal lords, and the peasants. Dick Robbins and I belonged to the peasants, and as kids we resented it. We could just feel all the wealthy people looking down at us in a kind of patronizing way. We didn't have the same advantages their kids had, private schools and Ivy League colleges. There was nothing in Wynwood for kids from our side of the tracks to look forward to, except serving the rich in one way or another. Then, when we were in high school, Dick and I ran into a character named Red Marvin." Quinlan chuckled. "When I say we 'ran into' Red, that's exactly how it was. We'd just won a football game, gotten a little high, and Dick ran a red light and smack into a passing trooper car. Red Marvin was the trooper driving it. He treated us less harshly than he might have, and we got to be friends. Red was a 'local' like us, but in his forties. He sympathized with Dick and me when we complained about the town—not wanting to leave it but also not wanting to be servants for the rich. There wasn't anything else. One thing more, Red told us. 'I don't have to tip my hat to anyone,' he said. 'The rich need the protection of the police, protection from vandals and burglars, and arsonists. Also, they have to be nice to us or risk speeding tickets and drunk-driving charges. So we are special. You want to stay in this neck of the woods, make a try for the state police. That way you can have your cake and eat it, too.' And he was right—except for Dick, who got it from some passing-through creep."

"You think he was shot by someone just passing through?" Peter asked. "I understood you to say he spotted a car coming out of one of the estates."

"People away," Quinlan said. "House dark, open invitation for a break-in."

"Someone just passing through would know or notice that?"

Quinlan frowned. "Because it was one of us who got it, we covered every possibility," he said. "Dick had reported on his car radio that he was following a black Lincoln-Mercury with a Connecticut plate. Only one plate on the rear in Connecticut. The plate was stolen off a Volkswagen somewhere else. We checked every dark-colored car in town that might have been mistaken for a Lincoln-Mercury. We questioned everyone living along the route who might have seen something. Complete blank. Bullets they dug out of Dick came from a .22 caliber handgun. We checked every gun we could find in town, guns owned by the rich and by the locals. Ballistics turned up nothing. You got a hunch about that, Styles? Something that tells you it was someone local?"

"No." Peter hesitated. "You think Dick Robbins was shot because he might have recognized the driver?"

"I think he was shot to avoid arrest," Quinlan said. "No more, no less. Perhaps there was stuff in the car—stolen goods, drugs, weapons, who knows? That's the kind of world we live in."

It was time to break it up. Peter rose to go, thanking his hostess for the drink and the cheese and crackers, and her time.

"I think you're a nice man to be concerned about Judith," Nora said. "I promise you, I'll get to her tomorrow sometime, give her a shoulder to cry on."

"One more thing," Peter said. "I somehow felt turned off by George Wilson. Judith ran right by him when I got her home, not stopping to tell him what had happened to her."

"What she *imagined* had happened," Quinlan said.

"That whole relationship is kind of twisted around," Nora said. "From all I hear Judith saw George Wilson as an interloper, the villain in that soap opera that was her life. She didn't blame her mother—couldn't, because she needed her mother."

"But what kind of man is Wilson really?" Peter asked.

"He was married before," Quinlan said. "Wife died of cancer. He and Rose Larsen were both lonely, both needed someone to fill a vacancy. I don't suppose either of them imagined Judith would react the way she did. From all accounts George tried very hard to win her over, but it hasn't worked."

"But what kind of a man is he?" Peter persisted.

"Local, high school education," Quinlan said. "Mowed lawns for people when he was a kid to earn pocket money. He was the only child in a churchgoing family. He was shrewd enough to see that he could set up a business that would service the whole community. It's worked out well for him, well for the big houses, the rich. He's provided jobs for a couple of dozen locals where there were no jobs before. Now he's a director of the local bank, deacon or whatever in the church. Solid citizen."

"That's what he's accomplished," Peter said, "but what kind of guy is he?"

"People who work for him respect him, trust him," Quinlan said.

"Mr. Styles is trying to understand why Judith passed Mr. Wilson by when he brought her home tonight," Nora said. "I think I can add something that may help. Wilson was a pleasant, cheerful, outgoing fellow until Rose had her accident. Since then he has been a grim, forbidding locked-in man. People understand the change, I guess. Rose just sits there, hour after hour, day after day, a nothing, a lump of flesh without any spark of life."

"A vegetable, Dr. Smalley called her."

Nora nodded. "I saw her quite often after Dick was killed. I went there to do what I could for Judith. Just looking at the poor woman made the hair rise on the back of my neck. No way you can blame George Wilson for turning bitter and hard."

"Dr. Smalley indicated he'd been generous with Judith."

"Put her through school," Nora said. "Her medical bills have been staggering since Dick was killed. When Dr. Kreuger suggested she should leave the area, go somewhere else, I understand Mr. Wilson volunteered to finance her until she could get started somewhere else. Judith refused flatly to go. Her mother might wake up some morning and know who she was and where she was."

"You've got to feel sorry for George," Quinlan said. "Living with one woman who's a nothing, and another who sees him as an intruder in his own house!"

"And Judith has no one to turn to, no one to share her troubles with," Peter said.

"Troubles, real or imaginary," Quinlan said.

It was going on two o'clock in the morning when Peter finally crawled into his comfortable bed at the camp. Sleep didn't come instantly. He tried to tell himself there was no reason for him to concern himself about the trials and tribulations of a probably severely neurotic girl. He had done everything a passerby could be expected to do. He had seen her safely home. He had reported the affair to the police. He had consulted with and alerted the girl's doctor. What else could be expected of him?

There are scenes in a good movie you remember long after the whole is forgotten, a moment of touching brilliance by an actor, a piece of photography that tells more than dialogue or action could do. Two moments in the evening stuck in Peter's mind as he lay awake staring at the ceiling in the dark. One was the look of terrible fear in Judith's eyes when she had burst in on him expecting to find a friend. Could he be trusted? Experience had evidently convinced her that there was no one she could trust. The other was when she had run up the path at George Wilson's house and brushed past her stepfather without a word. It suggested an unbearable aloneness better than any words could have explained it. He would, Peter thought, have stopped to attend to a wounded animal, stopped automatically. Would he pass by a human being wounded beyond endurance? Why not, when she had family, friends, doctors who knew her history, to care for her? There was no real reason for him to concern himself. George Wilson had said it was "their problem and they would attend to it." And yet . . .

He did sleep, finally. When he woke the sun was streaming in the windows and there was a new and beautiful day. There had been two incidents in Peter's own life, moments of violence, that had, he knew, brought him to the brink of madness. There had been a night long ago when he'd been forced off the road by some irresponsible kids and found himself lying some distance from the car he'd been driving, injured and helpless, while the car burned, his father trapped in it. Among the friends who helped Peter recover from that awful tragedy was a woman with whom he fell deeply in love. Not long after they had married, an assignment took Peter to the West Coast and his beloved Grace went with him. While he covered a lengthy trial Grace had helped out at a camp for Vietnamese refugees. One night some never-identified terrorists had invaded the camp, killing anyone who came into range of their automatic weapons. Grace was one of the victims of their senseless violence. Once again friends kept Peter from total self-destruction. His life was changed from the routines of investigative reporting to a crusade against violence and terror. But he had stayed in one piece because friends refused to let him throw in the towel. Judith Larsen evidently had no such staunch army of friends to turn to. Her father killed, her mother destroyed, her lover murdered, perhaps her rape story was a sick outcome of having to bear too much without anyone to turn to. Perhaps last night had been a second such demented fantasy. One thing was certain, however. The girl needed friends who could do more for her than try to persuade her she was out of her mind. Why Peter Styles? Perhaps because he was one of very few people she would ever find who had suffered the same kind of hammer blows to their sanity as she had. Perhaps if she could just tell her story and not see doubt in the listener's eyes she could find herself back to some sort of level keel. That couldn't cost him too much, Peter thought.

After a breakfast of juice, a couple of boiled eggs, toast, and coffee Peter walked out onto the camp's deck. The weather was a dream. Just beyond the camp's boathouse on the lake a boat with a scarlet sail moved slowly in the gentle breeze. The man in the stern saw Peter on the deck and waved to him. Peter waved back. It all seemed like the least likely place in the world to stage the kind of horror story Peter had heard the night before.

It was Peter's intention to drive up into town, make sure that George Wilson had gone to work, and then go to the house to look for Judith and offer himself as a willing listener. He didn't have to go as far as he'd expected to find her.

He drove his Toyota up to the main road, turned right to head for town, and there, on the left, in a piece of cleared ground he saw her. She was sitting there on top of a pile of what he saw were bricks and neatly stacked lumber. From where she sat she could look down over the tops of trees to the lake and the little scarlet sail zigzagging back and forth.

Peter parked his car beside the road and started to walk up into the clearing. Judith was instantly on her feet. She was, he thought, suddenly like a trapped animal crouching for an escape. He raised his hand and called out to her.

"No ski mask," he said. "It's Peter Styles."

She sank back down onto the pile of bricks and lumber and covered her face with her hands. He reached her and stood beside her, silent for a moment.

"Is this where you were last night when the man in the mask approached you?" he asked.

She nodded.

"And yet you come back."

She lowered her hands and looked up at him. Her eyes reflected an inner pain. "This was Dick's place. Now it's mine. I will *not* be frightened away! "

Peter gestured toward the bricks and lumber. "You were this close to beginning a house?"

"Dick planned to do a lot of the work himself," Judith said. "Look, Mr. Styles, you—"

"Peter," he said.

"By now you've been told I'm sick, imagining things that never happened. I warned you last night that it isn't healthy to get involved with me. It's the worst kind of bad luck."

"I don't believe much in luck," Peter said. "I was actually on my way to find you when I saw you sitting here."

"Find me to do what?" she asked.

"Listen—if you wanted to talk."

Her voice was bitter. "They didn't convince you?"

"I talked to Mike Quinlan and Nora, and Dr. Smalley. They're your friends."

"But they don't believe me," Judith said. "You also talked to my stepfather. He doesn't believe me either."

"Are you up to going through what happened last night?"

" 'Going through' ?"

"Show me where you were sitting when the man in the ski mask appeared."

"Right here, where I am now," Judith said.

"And the man in the mask came from where?"

She turned and pointed. "At the top of the clearing there."

"You could see him in the moonlight? No doubt about the mask?"

"No doubt. He called out to me. 'You crazy bitch, you'll never learn, will you!' He—he was coming toward me, not hurrying. I ran."

"Where did you run?"

"Down to the highway, across it, and down through the woods beyond it. Toward the Jordans' camp."

"You had walked down here from town? No car?"

"It was a lovely night. Dick and I used to come here on nights like that, planning—dreaming."

"You suggested that Bob and Betty Jordan were friends. You said they would believe you."

Her voice was unsteady. "The time before—when the

man attacked me. I went there—without any clothes—looking for help. They were out somewhere. The camp was locked. I couldn't find anything to cover myself—I couldn't get to their phone to ask someone to help me. The next day, the troopers were checking out my story and they went to see the Jordans. They had been out, of course, and Mike Quinlan found some of my bare foot marks in the flower bed outside one of the rear windows where I'd tried to get in that way. But the Jordans got the whole story from Mike—that I was probably off my rocker, that I'd invented the whole thing. Bob and Betty came to see me in the hospital where I was. They told me they believed me and would help any way they could. How could they help? The troopers and Dr. Smalley and Dr. Kreuger had made up their minds. But last night—I didn't know they'd gone to Europe and that you were in the camp. I went there because the Jordans were the only people who'd ever said they believed me."

"Could we walk out last night?" Peter said. "You show me exactly where you went? Most important, did he fire the shot at you up here in the clearing?"

"No. It was down in the woods on the other side of the main road."

"You didn't run down the driveway to the camp. Why the woods?"

"Because I thought I could take cover in the woods if I had to."

They walked down to the highway and across it.

"You were running, not walking like this," Peter said.

"Running for my life!" Judith said.

"And he behind you?"

"He—he used the road, shouting at me that I'd never make it. I think he knew where I was headed. He kept yelling at me to stop—calling me a 'silly bitch'!"

They had gone down through the well-cleared woods,

cared for, Peter remembered, by Maxi-Service, a couple of hundred yards.

"About here I—I tripped and fell," Judith said. She looked around as if looking for something to verify her story. "That's when he fired at me. I think I screamed."

"I think I heard that scream," Peter said. "I just thought it was kids having fun."

"Oh, my God," she said. "I thought I heard the bullet smack into a tree right beside me. I scrambled up and kept running. Through the trees I could see the lights on in the camp. I thought I had a chance and I made it. Only you were there, not the Jordans."

She started to move on down, but Peter's hand closed over her arm. "You say you heard the bullet smack into a tree?"

"Yes."

"You didn't look for it?"

"My God, Peter, I didn't think of anything but trying to get away from that lunatic! And it was dark! But I heard the sound of something hitting a tree very close to my head."

"And you had fallen—before the shot was fired?"

"Yes. He—the man—was cursing at me."

"Let's look," Peter said. "If you were stretched out on the ground and you thought the bullet hit very close to your head we need to look down low—a foot or two from the ground. You're sure this is the exact place?"

"I—I remember that little clump of birch trees," Judith said. "In the moonlight they looked like silver."

Peter moved slowly, looking down at his knee level at the trunks of trees, large and small.

"Got it!" he said, sharply.

About a foot and a half from the ground in the trunk of a sturdy oak tree was a fresh scar. He knelt down, touched the mark with his fingers. Imbedded in the wound he could feel the cool metal of the slug.

He stook up and looked at the girl whose eyes were wide as saucers. He smiled at her. "So it proves out, Judith. No more talk of fantasies," he said.

She stared at him for a moment, and then she rushed into his arms, crying uncontrollably. He held her, gently. If her story of last night was true then the odds were that her story of the rape was true. That being so, then the man in the ski mask was not some casual passer through town but someone permanently located in Wynwood. Someone, Peter thought, who might be watching them at this very moment, someone who might strike again.

3

"Months," Judith said, fighting to control her tears, "and nobody's believed a word I said!"

"You said the Jordans believed."

"I wasn't sure they did. They just wanted to be kind to me."

"Well, I believe and others are going to believe," Peter said. "We'll make 'em. Now—can you drive a car?"

She nodded. Peter took his car keys out of his pocket and handed them to her. "Take my car, go into town, and find Mike Quinlan. He's on a night shift, I think, so you'll probably find him at home. Get him here on the double. Don't tell anyone else what's happened except Mike. Keep looking for him till you find him."

"And you?" she asked.

"I'm staying here, just in case someone is watching us. I don't want anyone digging that bullet out of the tree but the police. Particularly no one but Mike Quinlan. He cares."

She still clung to him. "Oh, Peter, how can I ever thank you?"

He reached in his hip pocket and pulled out a clean linen handkerchief. He grinned at her. "Wipe your eyes, blow your nose, and get going. And don't talk to anyone except Mike."

She cut through the woods to the driveway, and he could hear her running up the hill to the highway. A moment later he heard his car motor start. He reached into his jacket pocket, took out a well-caked pipe, and filled it from a plastic pouch. He got it going with his lighter. All the while he was looking around him through the woods, watching for some sign of movement. There was nothing but a squirrel staring at him curiously from the branch of a tree, the twittering of birds, their privacy invaded. He glanced at his watch. It was just past nine o'clock. Working at night, there was a good chance Mike Quinlan would still be at home.

Peter sat down with his back to the wounded tree and waited. It was less than a half an hour when he heard two cars turn in the driveway at the top and start down. They stopped about level with where he was and Judith and Mike Quinlan, wearing civilian clothes, came through the woods to where he was waiting. Quinlan's usually relaxed, friendly face looked grim.

"Where is it?" he asked.

Peter stood up and pointed to the wound in the tree. "I didn't want to mess with it," he said. "I wanted you to see it the way we found it. It needs to be removed by someone official. Ballistics may tell you who owns the gun that fired it."

"Not likely," Quinlan said. He knelt beside the tree and felt the wound with his fingers. "It's a slug all right." He produced a heavy scout-type knife from his pocket.

"Don't scar it," Peter said.

Quinlan gave him a sour look. "Think I'm an idiot!" He dug a wide circle around the scar in the tree and pried out a chunk of wood with the bullet still embedded in it. He wrapped it in a handkerchief and stuffed it in the pocket of his blue denim jacket.

"Judith showed you where it was?" he asked Peter.

Peter sensed the other man's doubts. The whole damn town, he thought, had spent so long not believing Judith it wasn't going to be easy to sell them the truth. "I asked her to repeat her actions of last night," he said. "She was sitting up in her property when this creep in the ski mask appeared behind her. Bright moonlight. He threatened her, came toward her and she ran—down across the highway and through the woods here. The Jordans' camp was the nearest place where she thought she might get help. She tripped and fell, right here. The man was running down the driveway parallel to her course, shouting at her. When she fell he fired at her and she heard the bullet strike a tree. I looked around, thinking it must be low down if the man fired at a fallen figure—and there it was."

Quinlan looked at Judith. "You knew where it was? You saw it last night? You just wanted Peter to find it for himself?"

"No! No! No!"

"It occurs to me you may be setting Peter up," Quinlan said to the girl. "Getting a nice, friendly guy to fall for your story and back it up."

"Oh my God, Mike, *no*!"

Peter moved close to the girl and put a protective arm around her shaking shoulders. "Do you own a gun, Judith?"

"No!"

"Why don't you check out what that bullet has to tell you, Mike, before you try to make it tell you what you want to believe?" Peter asked.

Quinlan nodded, slowly. "I'm sorry, Judith," he said. "I'd like to believe. I really would. I'll take this slug up to the lab and see what it tells us. Don't get lost. I think Captain Stadler will want to talk to you and Peter."

They watched him make off through the woods to his car.

"It's been like that for so long," Judith almost whispered. "Anything I say they think I made it up."

"Well we're not going to wait till somebody kills you to prove to them that you're telling the truth," Peter said.

"Why, Peter? Why is someone bent on hurting me?"

"Let's go down to the camp," he said. "We can talk comfortably there."

They went out to where Judith had left the car and drove on down to the camp. The boat with the scarlet sail was still patrolling the lake just out beyond the boathouse dock. The sailor waved again and Peter waved back. Old friends without either of them knowing who the other was, Peter thought.

They sat out on the deck, watching the little sailboat tack back and forth, sipping the coffee Peter brought them in crockery mugs. It was a strange, soothing climate in which to be discussing violence.

"So no one has really believed you up to now, Luv," Peter said. "So no one has investigated things in a proper way. That's what we have to get to."

She gave him a quick, sideways glance. "You—you called me 'Luv,' " she said.

He smiled at her. "Miss Larsen and Judith both have a kind of formal sound," he said.

"Dick called me that—'Luv,' " she said.

"Sorry. I'll find something else."

"No—please. It—it makes me feel safe to be called that."

He turned his chair so that he was looking straight at her. "I know it's painful for you to talk about your first encounter with this character, but we've got to get some kind of lead to him. Wearing that ski mask, he could be fifteen or sixty."

"He is a big, very strong man," she said. "Not—not a kid."

"Nothing about him familiar—something you recognized in spite of the mask?"

"No. It—it was so quick, so violent."

"Can you tell me, knowing that I believe you?"

"Oh, Peter!"

"Easy does it."

She drew a deep, quavering breath. "After—after what happened to Dick I—I had just nothing left. My father was gone, my mother is nothing, God help her. I guess it's my fault that I could never accept my stepfather. He tried to take my father's place, but somehow that was—was repulsive to me. The thought of him making love to my mother—before she was hurt—was too much. I—I would lie in my bed and hear sounds coming from their room. I knew what was happening and I'd bury my face in my pillow to keep from screaming!"

"But your mother was happy?"

"Apparently—except for me. And then she was a nothing."

"Let's go back to the night you were attacked," Peter said.

"I'm sorry to wander," Judith said, "but it explains why I would wander down to Dick's property—my property now—just to be by myself with memories that were so very dear to me. There was no one to share them with."

"Mike Quinlan and his wife were friends."

"They were Dick's friends. The Jordans were just acquaintances until after—that night."

"No one else?"

She shook her head. "Before my father was killed I was just a kid. I was twelve when he died. I had school friends, but nothing with real roots. After Dad was gone I guess I was in a kind of shock. I couldn't share what I was feeling with anyone. I didn't want friends. I was just coming out of it when my mother married George Wilson. I should have been happy for her, but I wasn't. It was like a betrayal of my father. Maybe I am sick, Peter."

"It takes time to recover from any kind of knockout punch," Peter said.

"I couldn't seem to fit into my own generation," Judith

said. "In high school there was liquor, and drugs, and—and sex. I didn't want any of it. Liquor made me feel dizzy and out of control. I never tried drugs, although almost everyone else did—at least marijuana. And sex—well, I had some sort of old-fashioned idea. I would wait till someone I really loved came along. And he did come. Dick was everything I'd ever dreamed of."

"No sex with him?" Peter remembered Dr. Smalley's statement that she had been a virgin after the alleged rape—long after Dick was dead.

"He understood, and in a way it pleased him."

"And no boys before him?"

"No. I was propositioned. I guess I'm not—not unattractive, Peter."

"Of course you're not. You're damned attractive."

"But the word got around that I was a no-no girl and so there were no friends."

"Nobody who was angry at being rejected? No one who threatened you?"

"No."

"So that night, with Dick gone, you came down to your property?"

"It was a tie I had with someone I'd loved very much."

"Of course."

'I'd gone there many times, and that night was no different than any other—at first. I was sitting there, where you found me this morning, grieving over what I'd lost, what I'd never had, when suddenly he was there—the man in the ski mask. I hadn't heard him coming, and when I looked up I though it was some kind of joke—someone I knew playing a game with me." A tremor seized the girl's whole body for a moment. "Then he said, 'Take your clothes off.' I—I just didn't believe I'd heard what I'd heard."

"Recognize the voice?"

"No. I said, 'Who is it?' He said it again, loud and harsh. 'Take your clothes off.' I didn't move. I was suddenly cold with fear. Then—then he grabbed me, yanked me up to my feet, and began to tear at my clothes. I—it was a warm summer night. I just had on a cotton dress, panties. No bra, no stockings, just sandals on my feet. Suddenly I was naked and he was—was all over me. I—was down on the ground and he lifted the lower half of the mask and was at my mouth—his tongue—and a stubble of beard that rubbed my face raw—and later my breasts and my thighs. The people at the hospital thought it was all bramble scratches. It wasn't."

"You fought?"

She nodded, and tears had welled up into her eyes. "Afterward Dr. Smalley suggested it would all have been much easier if I'd just—let it happen. I don't know how to explain it, Peter, but I was—was trying to save something for someone who was already gone forever."

"Or who hasn't yet appeared on the scene," Peter said.

"It was instinctive, I guess. I struggled and clawed and scratched. I got away for a moment, but he caught up with me and we went tumbling into that clump of brambles—raspberry bushes I think they are. He was swearing, in that deep snarling voice. I think he'd hurt himself. I hoped I'd hurt him. That—that was when I got away again and ran on toward the Jordans."

"He followed you?"

"I think he did, but then he must have seen the lights up in the camp."

"I thought you said the Jordans weren't at home?"

"They weren't. But they'd left lights burning in the house. The man couldn't have known, unless he'd come all the way, that there wasn't help for me there."

"You never got a real look at his face, even when he lifted up the lower part of the mask?"

"Only that cruel mouth—and the stubble of beard. But he seemed like a giant at the time. So terribly strong—and yet clumsy."

"He swore at you then—the way he did last night?"

Judith shook her head. "He only spoke the one sentence to me—twice. 'Take your clothes off.' There was a lot of animal snarling and growling but no other words."

"But last night he talked a lot more. He said you were a crazy bitch, would never learn. And as he chased you he kept calling you a silly bitch?"

She nodded. Her face had a sudden pinched look to it.

"That first night, when you were fighting him off, were you aware that he was carrying a gun? He was all over you, you say. Did you feel something solid and hard against you, like a gun?"

"No." She reached a hand out to him. "Oh, Peter, I don't dare tell you what I thought last night. You, Mike, everyone else—would think I'm just as crazy as they've thought all along."

Peter looked at her steadily. "You thought it might not be the same man?"

"Oh, Peter!" She was suddenly on her knees beside her chair, clinging to him once more. "He seemed slimmer to me, more agile. His voice was higher pitched. But I thought—afterward—that the first time when I was being handled, thrown around, I was so terrified he'd seemed more monstrously big and strong than he really was. Who would believe there could be two men, wearing the same kind of ski mask, making the same kind of attack? I'd just be crazy Judith again!"

He reached out and stroked her reddish-brown hair gently. "I don't think you're crazy, Luv," he said. "I've had a lot of experience with violence and terror. I'll tell you about it sometime. More often than not it is the product of gangs, of groups. They don't need a real reason for what they do. One of them—someone local—knows your story. They see you going down to your property time after time. They decide to have at you. One of them attacks you. Then another. Go back to your place again tomorrow night and a third one might try. Fun and games!"

"Oh my God!"

"You don't sound crazy to me at all, Judith. And you've given us something concrete to look for. A gang of hoodlums located right here in Wynwood."

The number-one question, Peter knew, after being convinced that Judith was as sane as he was, was whether they were confronted by a gang of perverted young hoodlums preying on this one lonely, tragedy-struck girl, or whether there had been other similar incidents in the town or the general area, carefully concealed by protective families. There is no shame connected with being stabbed, or beaten, or shot at, or violently robbed; but let a girl be sexually molested and there is instantly something shameful about it. Perhaps, Peter thought, because it arouses shameful fantasies in other not-too-healthy minds. Perhaps because of ancient myths about chastity. Sexual attacks are kept hidden, too, for some practical reasons. In a small town like Wynwood the police would be close-mouthed about any incidents brought to their attention. Making them public might stir other sick minds into action. In Judith's case there'd been no way to keep it totally hidden. A naked girl stopping a car for assistance, taken to the hospital for attention, would have been about as easy to hide as an elephant in the middle of the village green. Succulent gossip, especially when the rumor must have leaked that it had probably never happened at all, demented behavior on the part of an unbalanced girl.

"Tell me, Judith," Peter asked the girl, "have you ever heard of any other activities by the ski-masked jerks?"

She shook her head. "No, but almost no one has ever talked to me about what happened. The word was out that I was mentally sick." Her laugh was bitter. "The only thing it was safe to talk about to me was the weather."

"Dr. Smalley? Dr. Kreuger?"

"Of course, they talked about it," Judith said. "Dr. Smalley kindly, Dr. Kreuger very clinically, but it was obvious they both had decided I'd dreamed the whole thing—tried in some crazy way to attract attention to myself."

"What about your stepfather?"

A cloud seemed to cross her face. "It—it was almost as if I'd done something deliberate to make him uncomfortable, unhappy. It—it would hurt his business! He asked me how I thought my mother must feel! Of course she isn't aware of anything that happens at all."

"And he knows that."

"I think he sometimes thinks that someday she'll 'wake up' and know everything he's ever said and done, everything that's happened while she was—the way she is. Of course, that's not so. All the doctors have made that quite clear to me."

"What about Mike Quinlan and his Nora—and the Jordans? You talked to them?"

"Mike, of course, has bought the police theory—that it never happened. They listened to me, patiently, kindly. They didn't try to persuade me I was crazy, but you didn't have to see it in print to know what they thought." Her smile was bitter. "They and the Jordans were the same. They were willing to help, to listen sympathetically, but they knew they were dealing with a—a scrambled egg!"

"Mike Quinlan mentioned a Captain Stadler."

"He's in command of the trooper barracks. He goes back a long way. He was a trooper when my father was killed. He was on patrol that night and was the first one to reach my father's burning truck. He was kind to me and my mother at the time. But as he's reached the top he's become a stiff, cold man. He was in charge of the investigation—that first time with the man in the ski mask."

"How did he handle it?"

"It was two or three days before I was able to be any help to them," Judith said. "Dr. Smalley told me I was in shock. Captain Stadler had the woods searched, but they didn't find anything helpful. When I was able they brought me out here and we went over the ground—much the way we just have this morning. Where was I when I first saw him? What happened then? They took me over every inch of the ground. They searched for my clothes and never found them. They decided that I'd dumped them in the stream and they'd been washed down into the lake. They even searched the lake, Mike told me."

"Quinlan was in on the investigation?"

"Captain Stadler thought I'd feel easier with Mike there. He'd been Dick's friend—and mine."

"You said you were wearing sandals that night."

"They were just slip-ons. They came off in the struggle I had with the man."

"That man took time to clean up the area, didn't he? Your clothes, your sandals, any evidence of his own presence."

"I guess he did. The only thing the troopers ever found to back up my story were my barefoot marks in the flower bed outside the back windows of this place." She looked past Peter toward the rear of the house. "Mike bought the conclusion they came to. That it was all some kind of nightmare."

"But I think he *is* your friend," Peter said.

"Trained to believe in evidence. And there wasn't any evidence."

"Except a naked girl crying out for help."

"A deranged naked girl," Judith said.

"When we're done with this you'll be swamped with apologies," Peter said. "To go back to what I asked you, Luv. Have you ever heard of any other stories of rapes in Wynwood?"

"You didn't go to high school with my generation, Peter. Who had to be raped? I am the only girl I know who always said no." She frowned. "I remember, after I'd come home from the hospital after the first time, Kay arguing with my stepfather."

"Who is Kay?"

"Oh—Kay Logan. She's the practical nurse who takes care of my mother. She lives in my stepfather's house with us. She's become like a member of the family."

"An argument with your stepfather?"

"He was saying that what I claimed had happened to me just couldn't happen in Wynwood. There'd never been a whisper of that kind of thing, he told Kay."

"All this in front of you?"

"No. But—but I heard. Kay is a great, big, hearty woman, blond, a little coarse sometimes. She—she loves an off-color joke. 'Every woman in the world has been raped at one time or another, George,' she told my stepfather. 'Even if it's only by her husband. When you don't feel like it you're being raped!' They both laughed. Then Kay admitted that she'd heard some rumors of young kids being attacked—when she was working in the hospital. 'Parents keep it quiet and the kids are taught to be ashamed,' she said. Then she laughed, that big, booming laugh of hers. 'You ever hear of anyone being raped in this town you better check out where Joel Kreuger was at the time. Every nurse in the hospital has fought him off—or given in to him.' "

"Joel Kreuger is Dr. Kreuger?" Peter asked.

Judith nodded. "My stepfather asked Kay whether she'd fought off Dr. Kreuger or given into him. Kay laughed again. 'I could take that creep with one arm tied behind me,' she said. 'He knew better than to try me.' "

Peter knocked out his pipe on the porch rail of the deck. "We'd better decide what our next move is," he said. "I'll drive you home and you stay there till we come up with some answers. If it should take a few days, don't come back down here to your property."

"You think—?"

"That's where they may hope to find you—these ski-mask characters."

"But *why* ?"

"You could represent a kind of challenge to them," Peter said. "They'll keep at it till one of them makes it."

There was nothing in the village of Wynwood to suggest any special excitement as Peter drove Judith along the main street and turned off toward George Wilson's establishment. There were eight or ten cars parked in the Maxi-Service yard, but Wilson's crew of men were obviously out on the job with their mowers, trucks, and other equipment. Peter drove up the rise of ground to the house and stopped near the front door.

"Just play it cool, Luv," he said, covering Judith's hand with his. "Very shortly the whole damn town is going to know that you've been telling the truth and that they have something very real to worry about."

"There's no way to tell you how grateful I am, Peter," Judith said.

"I needed help once and got it," Peter said. "Maybe helping you is one way of saying thanks. One day you'll have the chance to help someone else. That'll be your thanks."

She was looking past him toward the house and he felt her hand tighten on his wrist. "My mother and Kay Logan," she said.

Peter turned and saw a tall, big-bosomed blond woman

coming down the concrete path from the house, managing a wheelchair in which a dark-haired woman sat, staring down at the ground.

"Message for you, Judith," the big blond called out. "Captain Stadler wants you to stay put until he gets here." She looked at Peter. "This is Mr. Styles?"

"Yes," Judith said. "Kay Logan, Peter Styles."

"Heard about you," she said, held out her hand, and gave Peter a hearty, mannish handshake.

"I can't introduce you to my mother, Peter," Judith said. "She may or may not know you're here."

"We're down in the dumps today," Kay Logan said.

Peter was reminded of his own grim hospital experience and a cheerful nurse who would report to the doctor: "We've had our lunch, but we haven't been able to get much of a nap." It was as if she shared the experience, which in fact she did not. It was a technique for making him feel like an noncommunicating infant.

He looked down at Rose Wilson in the wheelchair. In spite of the warm summer day a woolen blanket covered her legs. She must, he thought, have been a very handsome young woman—high cheekbones, wide-set eyes, a broad mouth that must once have framed an attractive smile but was turned down at the corners now in a bitter expression. Hair that must once have been a rich chestnut color was a dull brown with a streak of white running up from the center of her forehead. Her whole face looked carved out of stone, rigid and fixed. He couldn't tell about the eyes because she never raised them from her steady stare at the ground. She simply wasn't here with them. How ghastly it must be for Judith to have a mother she loved turned into this rock-hard nothing.

"Stadler asked if you were here, Mr. Styles. I told him you weren't and he said if you turned up with Judith, please wait for him." She looked down at her stone-faced patient. "We're going to sit out on the terrace. The sun should help us get some color in our cheeks."

Just at that moment another car pulled up behind Peter's in the driveway. It was George Wilson. He came around to the side of Peter's car.

"I was in my office down below," he said. "I saw you drive up with Judith."

"She was down at her property. I gave her a lift," Peter said.

"Will you please help Kay with your mother, Judith," Wilson said to the girl. "I want to talk to Mr. Styles."

The girl gave Peter a frightened look, then got out of the car and stood by her mother's wheelchair.

"Here we go, up to the terrace," Kay Logan said.

Wilson watched them go, dark and scowling. When they were out of earshot he turned back to Peter. "I hoped I'd made it clear to you last night, Mr. Styles, that we have a problem we want to attend to ourselves."

"We?"

"My wife and I," Wilson said.

"That would seem to be a figure of speech, Wilson."

"I represent my wife, and I am responsible for Judith," Wilson said. "Apparently, she's sold you on this cockeyed story about a masked man. If there was any truth in it your help would be appreciated. As it is, you're getting into an act that's strictly for her doctors. It's dangerous for you, a stranger, to mess around in that girl's mind."

Peter opened his car door and got out, standing face to face with the angry Wilson.

"How would you feel, Wilson, if it turned out that Judith has been telling you the truth all along?" he asked.

"I'm not in the mood to play if-games with you, Styles. Perhaps I should thank you for being concerned, but I'm telling you to back off. Now, if you don't mind!"

"If you'll check out with Miss Logan," Peter said, "you'll

find that Captain Stadler has asked me to wait here until he arrives."

"Stadler's coming here?"

Peter nodded. "Let me tell you about this morning." He told of finding Judith on her property, their search through the woods for some kind of evidence, the lucky finding of the bullet embedded in the tree, and their involving Mike Quinlan in the situation. "So you see, it's quite possible Judith has been telling you the truth, right from the first rape incident six weeks ago. It's quite possible that bullet has told Stadler something."

"Judith told you where the bullet was?"

"She showed me where she was when it was fired," Peter said. "She heard it smack into a tree. It had to be close to where she said she fell before the shot was fired. It wasn't much of a trick to find it."

Wilson looked like a man who didn't believe a word of what he was being told.

"Are you a sucker for pretty young girls, Styles?" he asked.

Peter's smile was thin. "I'm a sucker for 'damsels in distress,' " he said.

Wilson turned away. "I'm up to here in damsels in distress," he said. "Maybe I should be glad to turn one of them over to you. I can't. I owe it to my wife to ride out Judith's problems with her, and I will. That doesn't include some stranger who sees a piece of white meat he thinks might come his way."

"I ought to be thinking about washing your mouth out with soap," Peter said very quietly. "But let me tell you that Judith and I have some things in common that she doesn't know about. Her father was in a car accident and was burned to death. So was mine. In my case I was driving the car, but I couldn't help him because my leg was crushed." Peter bent down, raised his right trouser leg and revealed the metal and plastic of an artificial leg. He straightened up, letting his pants leg drop. "Every time I strap that damn thing on in the morning I live it over again," he said. "Judith was in love with a man who was shot to death on the eve of their wedding by an unknown creep who's never been caught. I had a wife, my whole life, who was shot to death by terrorists who were just killing for the pleasure of it."

"My God!" Wilson said. "I remember reading somewhere—"

"It was everywhere to be read—to be seen on your television screen," Peter said, his voice grown harsh. "Perhaps that will help you understand why I have a special sympathy for Judith. There may not be anyone else in the world who has shared almost the exact same hammer blows."

"But you didn't go crazy afterward," Wilson said.

"I had friends who stood by, firm and strong. Judith didn't. But I have to tell you, Wilson, I don't think she went crazy either."

"Talk to Stadler when he gets here," Wilson said. "He'll tell you there wasn't a shred of evidence to back up her rape story."

"There was a bullet in a tree to back up her story of what happened last night," Peter said. "She's a twenty-year-old woman, Wilson. She needs help from someone who's prepared to believe her. I propose to give her that help if she'll take it. Somewhere in this sweet little town of yours there are people who need to be caught, convicted, and punished for what they've done to her. I intend to put that in motion even if no one else will."

"Are you suggesting there was something criminal about Kurt Larsen's death—her father's death?" Wilson asked, his face a dark thundercloud.

"I haven't had a chance to look into that yet," Peter said.

"For God's sake, Styles, that was a pure mechanical failure. Brakes on the truck gave out. Kurt couldn't make a curve halfway down Wynwood Mountain."

"Criminal or not, the effect on Judith was just the same. Then the accident to her mother. Then Dick Robbins. Of course, that dreadful sequence of events created an almost unbearable condition of shock. But the invention of further disasters? I don't believe it, and finding that bullet this morning has convinced me."

Wilson shook his head from side to side. "You haven't had to live with her, day after day. You haven't had to watch her go to pieces the way I have. No talk, wandering around the village at night like a lost soul, refusing to take the advice of her doctor. If you'd seen all that—"

"You're talking about Dr. Smalley?"

"Joel Kreuger. He's the local shrink. He's urged her to get away from this area for a while. He's tried to get me to persuade her. God knows she won't listen to me, and she won't listen to him. We've thought of trying to commit her, but old Doc Smalley fights that idea. Locking her up in an institution would just intensify the problem, he thinks."

"There seem to be some shreds of sanity somewhere," Peter said.

Wilson turned his head. "Here comes a trooper car now."

Sergeant Mike Quinlan, changed into his uniform, was driving the car with its searchlights on the roof. Sitting beside him was a slim, dark, deeply tanned man with a captain's insignia on his gray summer tunic. The two troopers left their car and came over toward Peter and Wilson. Coming across the lawn the gray-green eyes of the trooper captain were fixed on Peter, obviously trying to make some kind of assessment of a stranger. Mike Quinlan was completely deadpan. No one would have guessed that he and Peter, less than twelve hours ago, had shared drinks and talk together in Quinlan's house. He seemed to avoid looking at Peter.

"Morning, George," the trooper captain said to Wilson. Then he turned to Peter. "Mr. Styles? I'm Captain Stadler. Kay Logan told you I wanted to talk to you?"

"She did."

"Thanks for waiting," Stadler said. He turned back to Wilson. "I want to talk to Mr. Styles and Judith. Is there someplace we can be private?"

"Sitting room inside," Wilson said. He grinned. "Whole damn outdoors out here."

"I think I'd like to go inside," Stadler said. "I'd like to be near a telephone. I see Judith up there on the terrace with her mother. Ask her to join us, will you?"

The outside of George Wilson's house and its carefully tended lawns and flower beds had been no surprise to Peter. Healthy lawns, weedless garden plots, carefully trimmed shrubs and bushes were George Wilson's business, and he would certainly see to it that his own place was a good advertisement for potential customers. The inside of the house was something else again.

Most of the furniture that Peter saw as he went through an entrance hall and into a comfortable living room was American antique or excellent reproductions. Curtains and drapes had been bought by someone with taste. Somehow it didn't seem it could have been put together by a rough, tough fellow like Wilson. Either his first wife or Judith's mother had invested love and a knowledge of good things to make it all very special.

Stadler sat down in the corner of an upholstered bench that could have been an old church pew. He produced a notebook and pen from his pocket and George Wilson moved a little end table around in front of him.

"I can get Judith or Kay to make you some coffee, Frank," he said.

"Thanks, no," Stadler said. "But if you'll ask Judith to come in here, please." He gestured to Peter. "Sit down, Mr. Styles."

Peter sat in a comfortable armchair. Mike Quinlan, so far silent, stationed himself by the door as if to prevent anyone from coming in or leaving unexpectedly. Wilson had gone out through a glass door at the far end of the room that obviously led to the terrace. He came back at once with Judith in tow.

"Morning, Judith," Stadler said.

"Good morning, Captain."

"Just sit down over there and relax," Stadler said. "We've got some ground to cover."

Judith sat in a Windsor chair, stiff and straight. She gave Peter a quick glance, as if asking for help from him.

"I have a statement Mr. Styles gave to Sergeant Quinlan last night," Stadler said. "But it was secondhand, you understand—only what you told him. I'd like to hear it from you."

The girl's voice was unsteady. "You think I invented something again, don't you, Captain?"

"He can't," Peter said. "There's the bullet. He's got it."

Stadler wasn't pleased. "I'd appreciate your letting me do the questioning, Styles. Now, tell me, Judith, how it was. You went down to that property of yours after dark?"

"It was a beautiful, bright, moonlit night," Judith said. "Almost like daylight."

"It seems strange to me that after what you say happened there six weeks ago you'd go down there again at night," Stadler said.

"It—it's a place where I have something private, something personal and precious," the girl said. "I supposed the other man was long gone by now."

"The other man?"

"The one who attacked me."

"So you went there last night, not afraid it would happen again. What did happen?"

Judith took a deep breath and began with the man in the ski mask appearing above her in the clearing. "You crazy bitch, you'll never learn, will you?" Her flight down through the woods with the man following down the parallel road, shouting at her that she was a "silly bitch"—her fall, the shot, the sound of the bullet smacking into the tree near her head, her running on down to the Jordans' camp and finding Peter there.

"He didn't follow you after he'd fired the shot?" Stadler asked.

"I—I don't know," Judith said. "I could see the lights in the camp down below me through the trees. I—I just started running there, shouting for help. I was making so much noise myself I might not have heard him on the road."

"When he saw the lights on in the camp he probably gave up," Peter said.

"Please, Mr. Styles!" Stadler said. "You reached the camp, Judith, without seeing or hearing this man again? He didn't shout at you or curse at you again?"

"I—I didn't hear him if he did. I—I was afraid for my life, Captain. All I could think of was reaching the camp where I thought I'd find friends and help."

"And instead of those friends you found Mr. Styles?"

"Yes."

Stadler turned to Peter. "And you, Mr. Styles, you were sitting there in the peace and quiet of a summer night and you didn't hear any of this? In your statement to Sergeant Quinlan you said you didn't hear the shot."

"I didn't," Peter said. "A small-caliber handgun wouldn't make much noise a hundred yards away. I had my radio on, I think, listening to a news broadcast. I did hear a woman scream."

"And thought it was kids, playing games," Stadler said, referring to his notes.

"Something like that."

"So Judith burst into the house where you were and told you her story?"

"She told me some of it, not all at that time."

"Did you go looking for the man she said had attacked her, shot at her?"

"No," Peter said.

"Afraid?" Stadler asked, his eyes narrowed.

"Just sensible," Peter said, smiling at him. "I listened at the door, didn't hear anything or see anything. I was concerned for Judith, who was in a hysterical state. When I got her quieted down I thought the best thing was to get her home to her friends and family."

"You didn't think this guy might take a shot at you when you went out to your car? You weren't afraid to run that kind of risk?"

"It seemed wise not to stay set up there," Peter said. "Whoever it was wasn't after me, he was after Judith. Getting her back here to her family seemed to be what I had to do."

"And no sign of the man when you drove out?"

"No. I got her back here and to her stepfather. Then I went straight to the barracks and reported what had happened."

"And Sergeant Quinlan sent you to see Dr. Smalley and you found out you might have been sold a nightmare?"

"I had a hunch it was no nightmare," Peter said. "This morning I found out I was right. I found Judith up on her property again and we walked out the pattern of last night. I found the bullet, and sent Judith for Sergeant Quinlan to take charge of it. Incidentally, Captain, there's one thing Judith hasn't told you."

"Oh?"

"She doesn't believe last night's man with the gun is the same man who attacked her six weeks ago. Slimmer, more agile, not so big a man. That makes it sound like a gang or group of young creeps."

Stadler's face was granite hard. "There's something you don't know, Mr. Styles. You're entitled to know since you found us that bullet. Ballistics! We didn't expect to find anything. There's hundreds of .22 guns all over the country. But we ran into something in our records right off the bat. Take a guess."

"You know who owns the gun," Peter said.

"I wish to God we did," Stadler said. "What we do know is that the gun that fired that bullet you found in the tree is the same gun that was used to shoot down Dick Robbins."

There was a little gasping cry from Judith.

"The man who fired that shot into the tree may be a murderer we've been looking for for months! At least he had the murderer's gun, and, by God, we're going to find him! Dick Robbins was one of us!"

What Stadler wanted from Judith were facts about last night's man, the one who had fired the shot. The facts he wanted the girl couldn't really supply. A description? The brief look she had of him coming toward her from the upper edge of the clearing produced nothing helpful. The ski mask—yes, just like the one the man had worn six weeks ago, the bigger man—brown, with two holes for the eyes, a slit for the mouth. Was he dark or fair? No way to tell with his head covered. His size? About as tall as Mike Quinlan, Judith guessed; perhaps not quite so rugged, so heavy. That translated for Stadler into five feet ten, about a hundred and sixty pounds. Clothes? Judith thought blue jeans, a dark shirt, black or navy blue. No jacket. It had been a pleasantly warm night. Shoes? She hadn't noticed. Did he show the gun, was he carrying it openly, when she first saw him? When she heard him speak, somewhat muffled by the mask, she hadn't thought of anything but getting away. Did he try to stop her by threatening to shoot? She'd run the moment she saw him. He'd been shouting something after her, but she hadn't heard the words. She hadn't even thought of a gun until she tripped, fell, and heard the shot fired and the bullet whistle past her head.

"You got up and ran again?" Stadler asked.

"Yes."

"And you don't know if he followed you on down the drive?"

"I was yelling for help, Captain. I knew someone was at the camp. I—I was breathless, making quite a bit of noise as I scrambled through the woods. I—I just don't know if he followed."

Stadler turned to Peter. "You say you went to the door and looked and listened, Styles."

"Nothing," Peter said. "You've got yourself an interesting situation, Captain. A man who committed a murder months ago is still here in your own backyard. He wasn't a passing thief. Since Robbins started to walk up to his car after he'd stopped him, the chances are he knew the driver. The same guy and at least one friend have some reason for harassing Judith. Why? They know where to find her when they want to give her a bad time. You've got a local horror stew cooking on your own front burner."

"Thanks for telling me," Stadler said.

"It's hard to believe," George Wilson said, speaking for the first time. He had been standing by the glass door leading out to the terrace. "There's no such thing as a stranger in this town, except a salesman passing through. And we know all of them."

"That really isn't a very realistic statement, is it, Wilson?" Peter asked. "You have a community with dozens of big estates in it. These wealthy people have guests, out-of-town members of the family who are repeat visitors. You have a hospital that services the county. More strangers than in the average small community come and go."

"I guess I was just thinking of the people you see every day," Wilson said.

Stadler was scowling at his note book. "As a matter of fact, you're a stranger, Styles," he said.

"But a lucky one." Peter said. "At the time Trooper Robbins was murdered I was on assignment in the Middle East—Cairo, as a matter of fact. Six weeks ago when Judith was first attacked I was in London. That's where I ran into Bob and Betty Jordan, old friends, on the first leg of their summer abroad. That's when they told me I could have their camp for the summer. Last night? Well, I was here last night, but I doubt very much you think seriously of me as a suspect."

"We don't have anything on you so far, Styles," Stadler said.

"That's nice to know," Peter said. "Last night I found myself believing most of what Judith told me. Today I believe her entire story. That brings me to something else I have to tell, Captain. What we have is murder and terror in a small New England town. That's my beat as a professional reporter. So I'm no longer just here to try to get started on a book. Now I'm here as a reporter, looking for the truth."

Stadler pushed aside his table and stood up. He was angry. "In that case, Styles, you're not entitled to be present at a preliminary investigation. So take off!"

Peter moved over to where Judith was sitting and put his hands on her shoulder. "Take it easy, Luv," he said. "You know where to reach me if you need me. And I'll be in touch."

"Oh, Peter, thank you, thank you so very much!"

Sergeant Quinlan opened the outside door for him and spoke under his breath. "The captain has a short fuse, but he's a good man."

"I'll try to remember," Peter said.

He had a kind of sympathy for the short-fused Stadler as he drove down from the house, through the Maxi-Service yard, and out onto the village street beyond. Much of Peter's career had been involved with police, from village sheriffs to Interpol on the international scene. One of the problems for the law, on any level, is the press. They can't be ignored, the public has a right to the information they go after, but there are many times when, if the press could be kept out of the picture, a criminal would not be forewarned of what the police knew and escape a trap into which he might otherwise have fallen. Stadler was probably kicking himself now for having let anyone know that the bullet found in the tree had come from the same gun that had murdered Dick Robbins. He was probably kicking himself extra hard for letting Peter, a reporter for a national magazine, know. Wynwood, quiet in its way, would suddenly attract reporters, radio and television newsmen, feature writers from all over the country when the story of murder and terror broke. Some of the great private fortunes in America were located there. Peter wondered how long he could hold off on the essential fact about the bullet so that the murderer wouldn't dispose of his gun and go whistling in safety along Wynwood's village green.

As he drove along that village green Peter saw Dr. Smalley standing by the garden gate outside his house in conversation with a young man who looked about college age. Peter waved, and instantly the doctor signaled him to stop. The old man and his young friend came quickly out to the curb where Peter pulled in his Toyota.

"Speak of the devil," Dr. Smalley said. "This is Ben Gleason, Peter Styles."

"It's great to meet you, Mr. Styles," the young man said. He was fair, bright-eyed, dressed casually in khaki slacks and a plaid sports shirt, blue running sneakers.

"Ben is a reporter for our local scandal sheet, the *County Advocate*," Dr. Smalley said. "He was just asking me if I knew how to find you."

"You've been a role model for me ever since I started working on a paper, Mr. Styles," Gleason said. "I've been planning to set up a chance to just chat when I heard you were here in town for the summer. Then, a little while ago, the roof blew off!"

"I hadn't noticed," Peter said, smiling at Gleason.

"I was at the barracks when they got the report from ballistics about the bullet you found in a tree outside your camp, Mr. Styles," Gleason said. "You haven't just come from the camp, have you?"

"No. Why?"

"When I heard the bullet had come from the gun that was used to kill Dick Robbins I wanted more of the story than I could get from Stadler or Mike Quinlan. I drove down to the Jordans' camp, looking for you. There was no sign of you, but the front door was open. I thought I'd leave a note for you, asking you to call me when you could. My God, Mr. Styles, the place is a shambles."

"How do you mean, shambles?"

"Torn apart," Gleason said. "Your typewriter smashed on the fireplace hearth; notes and papers torn up and scattered around like snow. I thought you might be somewhere inside, hurt. Someone violent had been there and might have attacked you. In your bedroom I saw clothes—slacks, jackets, shirts—torn up, scattered around. I went back into the front of the house and called the barracks to tell them what I'd found. Neither Stadler nor Mike Quinlan were there. I left word with the man on the desk to locate them and tell them what I'd found."

Peter's face had turned gaunt and hard. "They're both up at George Wilson's place. I just left there," he said.

"When I put down the phone—there in the camp—I saw the note for the first time. It was taped to the mantel," Gleason said. "Looked like it had been written with some kind of a marker pencil—thick, black strokes. I left it where it was, but it said: 'STYLES—WHY DON'T YOU GET OUT OF TOWN AND MIND YOUR OWN BUSINESS?' "

"Let's go down and have a look," Peter said.

"Hadn't you better wait for the troopers?" Dr. Smalley asked.

"I don't scare easily, Doctor," Peter said. "By the way, Judith Larsen is as sane as you or me—maybe saner. Riding with me, Ben, or have you got your own wheels?"

"I'm with you, Mr. Styles, all the way!" the young reporter said, scrambling into the Toyota's passenger seat beside Peter.

PART TWO

1

Shambles was almost a gentle word for what Peter found at the camp. Vandalism wasn't new to him. He had seen the desecration of a synagogue in Manhattan, the careful destruction of equipment in a high school on Long Island, the senseless graffiti applied to art works in a museum in the Midwest. He had always felt there was a kind of jeering humor connected to those things he'd seen. Here, in the camp, was the signature of some kind of white-hot rage.

Peter parked the Toyota at the front of the house and he and young Gleason went up onto the deck together. There was no visible damage to the house itself.

"Let's be careful not to smudge fingerprints," Peter said. "Did you handle this front screen door, Ben?"

"Afraid I did," young Gleason said. "You know, the inside door was open and I could look inside. I called out to you. When you didn't answer I thought there was no reason I couldn't step inside and leave you a note. So—I opened the screen door. The way the sun was, Mr. Styles, I couldn't really see inside till I *was* inside!"

Peter opened the screen door and went in. The first thing he saw was his portable typewriter smashed down on the stones of the fireplace hearth. He didn't need to examine it to know it was wrecked beyond repair. A later look showed that it must have been hurled down on the stones, picked up, hurled down again—and a third time to make absolutely certain it was destroyed. It was like seeing an old friend dead in an accident. That typewriter had been with Peter a long time, most recently in Cairo where he'd covered the aftermath of the assassination of Anwar el-Sadat, Egypt's president. More recently it had been with him in London where he'd used it to report on the death of a British diplomat in a bombing, presumably by Northern Irish terrorists. It had stared at him reproachfully during yesterday's attempts to get his novel started. An old and trusted friend. Peter could feel a scalding anger rising in him that had been a reaction to other violences in his life.

The torn-up papers scattered around "like snow" didn't represent any serious loss. They had been notes and a few abortive paragraphs he'd typed out in an effort to get started on his book. But they were part of the destructive fury so eloquently testified to by the destroyed typewriter.

He paused to look at the note taped to the fireplace mantel. The paper had been taken from his supply. As young Gleason had suggested it appeared to have been written with a marker pencil of some sort. It was printed, crudely as if by a small child. "STYLES—WHY DON'T YOU GET OUT OF TOWN AND MIND YOUR OWN BUSINESS?"

"The bedroom is the only other place," Ben Gleason said.

Peter walked down the hall to the place where he slept. There two summer tweed jackets, several pairs of slacks, his shirts, underclothes, and handkerchiefs had been torn and ripped to shreds and piled on the bed. He stepped into the adjoining bathroom. The black marker had been put to use again on the mirror over the washbasin. "GO HOME!" His shaving equipment, toothbrush and paste, hairbrush and comb had been thrown on the tile floor and apparently jumped on. Peter thought, grimly, that if he were to stay here he would have to completely reequip himself. The man responsible for this had made certain he had nothing personal left intact. Nothing belonging to the Jordans in the rest of the house had been touched.

As he returned to the living room Peter saw young Gleason bending down to pick up the shattered typewriter.

"Don't touch that, Ben," he said, sharply. "If anything will take prints that machine will."

Gleason straightened up. "Sorry. Somehow it was like leaving someone hurt unattended."

"I know. I feel the same way. Let's wait for the troopers out on the deck. That way we won't risk messing up anything that might be helpful."

The two men went outside. Out on the lake Peter saw his old friend, the navigator in the little boat with the red sail. The man in the boat waved as he had on other occasions and Peter waved back.

"That's Bill Steele," Gleason said. "His father is Cyrus Steele. He owns one of the big computer companies—Steele Business Machines. Boy, are they loaded! They own a big place out on Route Seven. The old man gave a million bucks to help build the local hospital."

"He seems to own this end of the lake," Peter said.

"He could afford to buy it if he wanted it," Ben said. "Why would anyone do this to you, Mr. Styles?"

"Let me ask you a question first," Peter said. "You say you were at the barracks when they came up with the ballistics report."

"I was. I was there, just checking out the police blotter for news, when Mike Quinlan came in with the bullet you'd found in the tree. They didn't expect it would prove out anything, but I stuck around. Mike Quinlan and I—and Dick Robbins, by the way—went to school together. Like I say, I hung around, and suddenly Mike reappeared and told me they'd struck gold the first time around. The bullet came from the gun that killed Dick. Boy, did I have a story."

"He didn't ask you to keep it quiet?"

"Mike didn't. I hot-footed back to my boss at the *Advocate* and told him what I had."

"Your boss is—?"

"Brad Smith. He owns the *Advocate*, edits it, runs it. He did what was normal in the situation. He phoned in the story to the national news service we use. A little after he'd done that Captain Stadler called in and said he'd appreciate it if we didn't release the story. It was too late."

"So the press and the media are going to be swarming all over us."

"Likely," Gleason said. "There are so many important names and so much money in this town. Anything sensational happens there and it'll draw more than flies. Anyway, Brad told me to find you and get your side of the story about finding the bullet. I tried you on the phone, and when you didn't answer I came down here to leave you some kind of a message." He gestured toward the screen door. "I found that."

It explained, Peter thought, why Stadler had been willing to talk about the bullet. It was too late to keep it a secret. It must have burned him that Mike Quinlan hadn't thought to tell his friend to keep the information off the record.

"How did the *Advocate* handle the story of the attempted rape of Judith Larsen—when was it, six weeks ago?"

"It didn't break at all at the time," Gleason said. "You've heard it? How Mike Quinlan, on patrol, was flagged down by Judith, stark naked, waving a tree branch? Well, Mike took her straight to Dr. Smalley. She was too hysterical to tell her story, I guess. Anyway, Dr. Smalley thought it wasn't a police case until Judith could tell them exactly what happened. I guess everybody played along with Doc Smalley. He's well liked, trusted, been the town doctor forever. We didn't even get wind of it at the time. I guess Doc Smalley, and later Dr. Kreuger at the clinic, decided that what Judith was telling them had never really happened. But after a week or so the story did get out. Maybe nurses at the clinic started it, maybe friends of Judith's who came to see her when she was convalescing from whatever had or hadn't happened. I heard it and I went to Brad Smith and told him there might be a story. Either way, fact or fiction, it was a story."

"I understood the troopers had acted," Peter said.

"Searched the area, couldn't find any evidence, couldn't find Judith's clothes."

"I guess they did, and I guess that contributed to the diagnosis the two doctors made—all a psychic disturbance, never happened. A small-town weekly newspaper isn't like a big-city daily, or a national magazine like your *Newsview*. We don't always print a story if it will cause someone pain or distress. There wasn't any story here except that a local girl had been picked up, naked, by a patrolling trooper. There wasn't any factual story to follow up. If the *Advocate* printed what we had, it would make Judith what Brad Smith calls a 'finger-pointing victim,' probably for the rest of her life, or as long as she lived in Wynwood. So it was pushed onto a back burner. Now, of course, it will all come out because we have three stories—a murder, a rape, a second attack on Judith—and this vandalism, which seem to be related. I mean, they have to be related, don't they, Mr. Styles? There isn't any other reason for someone to raise that kind of hell with your things?"

"There isn't any other reason for wanting me to leave town," Peter said. "I started last night, before we found the bullet, to persuade Dr. Smalley and Sergeant Quinlan—and his wife—that Judith was telling the truth, not only about last night but about the rape incident."

"You believed her from the start?"

"A hunch, Ben. Someday, when you've been at this business as long as I have, you'll start believing in your hunches."

"You're going to stay and cover the story till you get to the bottom of all this, aren't you, Mr. Styles?"

"You can count on it."

"Could we—do you think we could work together on it? You could probably teach me more in a day than I could learn in a year."

Peter smiled at him. "How could I get along without you, Ben? You know the town, and that's where it's all at."

A few minutes after that the troopers did move in. Captain Stadler and three other men came in two cars. One of the troopers was a fingerprint expert and he began going over everything that had been touched by the vandals. There wasn't much result from any questions Stadler could ask. The camp and its contents had been intact when Peter and Judith had left after Sergeant Quinlan had pried the bullet out of the tree in the woods and taken it to the barracks. The question as to whether Peter had locked the front door when he and Judith headed back to George Wilson's couldn't be answered. There was an automatic lock on the door—a button you push that makes the catch unworkable from the outside. Peter remembered checking it when he'd first gone up the hill and had found Judith sitting on the pile of materials on her property. He'd unlocked it with his key when he and the girl had come back down after Quinlan had come and gone. He didn't recall touching the lock button after that, so the door should have been locked. But there was no sign of any sort of break-in. Who had another key to that front door? Peter knew of no one, had been told of no one by the Jordans.

"They'd cabled a Mrs. Summers who's a local real estate agent," he told Stadler. "She had a key to the camp and she turned it over to me when I arrived. It's here, on the ring with my car keys."

"Diane Summers," Stadler said. "She may know if someone else had a key."

The trooper captain asked the right questions. Who else did Peter know in town? There had been no one until last night. His intention, when he'd arrived four days ago, was to make no local contacts at first. He wanted to get launched on his book without any interference from well-meaning neighbors or possible celebrity hunters. He hadn't met anyone, talked to anyone, except the postmaster with instructions about his mail, until last night when Judith came bursting in on him. After that there had been

George Wilson, Sergeant Quinlan at the barracks, Dr. Smalley, and then Quinlan's wife, Nora. Today there'd been Rose Wilson, Kay Logan, the practical nurse, and finally Ben Gleason.

"All in the last fourteen hours, the sum total of all the people I know by sight in Wynwood."

"Plus Diane Summers and the postmaster—that'd be Fred Kleeman, unless you talked to one of the clerks," Stadler said.

"Big man with red hair," Peter said.

"That's Fred Kleeman." Stadler put away his notebook. "Well, you're not going to be able to walk down the main street now without being swarmed over, Styles. Thanks to young Gleason here being so quick on the trigger, the whole damn world knows what's going on in Wynwood now."

The troopers took Peter's fingerprints so they could separate them from any others they might find on his belongings. The destruction had been so complete. There were things Peter hadn't noticed at first glance. The Mr. Coffee machine, tossed on the floor, its glass ball broken; liquor emptied out of bottles; liquid, probably coffee, poured into a fresh tin of pipe tobacco. Two pairs of shoes missing—found later where they'd been thrown out a window into the woods. Nothing that represented any kind of personal living comfort for the Jordans' tenant had been left undamaged or untouched.

"Looks like you'd have to leave town, just go get yourself a clean handkerchief," Stadler said.

"You might be surprised," Peter said. "I'm not leaving town until we get the sonofabitch who's responsible for this, Captain. And for God knows what else!"

Stadler gave him a steady look. "I guess we're stuck with you," he said. "Don't try to be a hero, Styles. We're dealing with someone who plays for keeps. And if you come on anything, don't stay private with it. We can't help you if you try to be a boy wonder."

The troopers left after that, taking everything with them the vandal or vandals had handled. Ben Gleason stayed behind, bright-eyed, waiting for Peter to tell him what their next move should be. The young reporter could be a help, Peter thought, but he could also be a damned nuisance.

There were things Peter had to do for himself. A call to New York put him in touch with the woman who cleaned his apartment for him there. She had a key to the apartment and he gave her a list of things he wanted packed—clothes mainly. By the time she'd done what he asked, someone from *Newsview* would show up to get the things he wanted and bring them to him.

Then he called Frank Devery, his editor, boss, and friend at *Newsview*. Devery was already aware of part of the story. News services had most of it except, of course, the vandalism at the camp.

"I'd have bet on it, chum," Devery said. "You'd find something to prevent your doing what you went up there to do. How many pages you got on the book?"

"Zero," Peter said. He told his friend about the vandalism, and asked to have someone sent to pick up clothes for him. "Mrs. Pomeroy will have them ready."

"I'll bring 'em myself," Devery said. "I'd like to have a look at that gold-plated village. I take it you want to cover the story?"

"You know it."

"I should get there early in the afternoon," Devery said. "Where will you be?"

"The *County Advocate* is the local newspaper," Peter said. "Ask there. Someone will know."

"I dare say there'll be a neon sign somewhere pointing to you," Devery said. "If I was a local community I'd bar you."

He chuckled. "Wherever you go, chum, there's always hell to pay."

"Which is why you hired me," Peter said.

Young Ben Gleason was waiting impatiently for the phone calls to be finished. As soon as Peter had hung up on Devery he asked if Peter planned to go talk to Brad Smith, the editor of the local paper. "You said they'd know where you were."

"First thing a good reporter does in a strange town is talk to the local peers in his business."

"I know Brad will be delighted to meet you," Gleason said.

Brad Smith was a pleasant surprise. A big, shaggy, gray-haired, pipe-smoking man. Smith's tanned face was deeply creased, lines etched there by humor and compassion, Peter thought. His greeting was hearty, his handshake firm and warm.

"You've had a kind of tough introduction to New England's gold coast, Mr. Styles," he said. "I don't mind telling you it's an honor to have you here. I've followed your columns for what—ten, twelve years? You like to think the things you write about won't happen in your world, but they do. It's all around you."

Ben and Peter were in Smith's little private office off the main office space of the *Advocate*. The editor's desk was a littered confusion, but Peter imagined Smith could reach out and find anything he wanted without any hesitation. The big man, constantly relighting a pipe that didn't seem to draw properly, listened to the story of the vandalism at the camp.

"You'd think of a thing like that as being the work of kids, wouldn't you?" Smith said. "The world isn't what it used to be Mr. Styles. I've come to believe that, these days, when you talk about adolescents you're talking about anyone from the age of ten to the age of thirty."

"Thirty!"

Smith nodded. "They don't grow up when they should, they don't get on their own. There's no woodshed anymore, no discipline. Young people expect and demand support and acquiescence long past a reasonable time. Drugs, liquor, sex—all considered routine by today's young people. They expect to be allowed to indulge, get away with it, and to hell with the consequences. Parents stay blind to it. 'Not my kid!' they tell themselves. It's always the other fellow's kid. It's specially true in our little gold-plated cesspool."

"You surprise me," Peter said. "I thought of Wynwood as a safe, secure, completely peaceful place."

"Until last night?" Smith suggested. "You probably never worked on a small-town paper, Mr. Styles. We have a different set of ethics than the press in a big city. I almost said 'the outside world.' I think Ben will tell you we suppress more local stories than we print. Preserve an image, I guess, the name of the game. We tell ourselves that it's a kindness not to print scandals about local people. You want the truth? It's really fear, not kindness at all."

"You're telling me that you're afraid to print the truth?"

Smith knocked out his pipe and reached for another one in a china bowl on his desk. He began stuffing it from an open tin of tobacco with his strong, square fingers. He didn't look like a man who lived with fear.

"You walk into this town, Mr. Styles, and you're confronted by a terrified girl who claims she's been attacked by some hoodlum in a ski mask. You believe it. Why not? But instantly you're told by the girl's stepfather that she's off her rocker. The local cops imply the same thing and send you to the local doctor to back up that story. What more do you need to be convinced that you've helped out a sick girl and that it's not your problem. But, because you're not from this world, you don't let go. This morning you prove that maybe she isn't crazy. So now you get an outright warning. Get out of town or else. So I take it you're not going."

"I'm not."

"What do you expect will happen next?"

"Happen?"

"They're not done with you, Mr. Styles, if you don't go. Or at least lay off!"

"You keep saying 'they.' "

"It's a guess," Smith said. "I suspect you've made the same guess. You think two different men attacked Judith Larsen—the rape case six weeks ago and last night."

"How do you know that?"

"All the people who report to me don't wear press badges," Smith said. "I know something about what you told Stadler up at George Wilson's place earlier today. A big giant of a man in the rape case; a smaller, more agile man last night."

"You're getting away from what you said earlier—that you suppress stories out of fear, not compassion. Ben told me you didn't print the story about the rape incident because you believed the doctors and you didn't want to put Judith in the position of being pointed at for the rest of her life."

"If I could have proved her story I'd have printed it," Smith said. "Do you know that ten minutes after Mike Quinlan took naked Judith Larsen to Dr. Smalley's that night six weeks ago I had a call from the doctor. 'You're going to hear that someone tried to rape Judith Larsen,' he told me. 'I don't believe it's so. Just lay off it, will you Brad, until I can get to the bottom of it? If you print her story all it will do will make her an object of scorn. She's a very sick girl.' "

"And that intimidated you?"

"Let me say this to you, Mr. Styles, it made me hold off

for the time being. Oh, we worked on the story. Ben, here, is a school friend of Mike Quinlan's. He got the facts about being flagged down by the naked girl from Mike. But I kept it out of print because—well, if she was sick—"

"That's not the only reason, is it?"

"Ben found out the police had covered the whole area where Judith said it happened. Nothing. No sign of her clothes. It looked more and more like a sick drama made up by a sick girl."

"But that isn't why you didn't print it?"

"You really stick to it, don't you, Styles? I guess that's the difference between the bush leagues and the big leagues." Smith reached out and picked up a copy of the *County Advocate*. He turned to an inside page, refolded the paper and handed it to Peter. What was there was a full-page ad for "MAXI-SERVICE, George Wilson, Mgr."

"Fifty-two weeks a year," Brad Smith said. "Two hundred bucks a week. That's a lot of capital to lose in this kind of operation just to satisfy your conscience as a reporter."

"But a naked girl did flag down a patrolling cop. That's a story, whatever happened," Peter said.

"You live in the instant world of radio, television, wire services, three or four editions of a daily paper. You print what comes over the line and never mind how it turns out. Working on a weekly is a little different," Smith said. "We get wind of something on a Thursday. That's the day we come out, so no way a story can appear this week. That gives us till the following Wednesday to decide if we have a story. That's how it was in Judith Larsen's case. It happened on a Thursday."

"Friday," Ben Gleason said.

"So we had five days we could take to decide. By that time Doc Smalley and Dr. Kreuger convinced me we were dealing with a sick girl, so why hurt her?"

"And there was ten thousand dollars' worth of advertising," Peter said, pointing to the paper he was still holding.

Smith gave him a tired smile. "The ingredients of a decision," he said. "Now we're going to be running after the big boys, like you, Mr. Styles, with our tongues hanging out, trying to catch up with the rest of the world." He pointed toward the outer office. "Our phone has been ringing steadily for the last hour, calls from newspapers, wire services, radio and TV stations. We're the local news source. What are the facts? What did we print about the murder of a trooper six months ago? What did we print about a rape case six weeks ago? What happened last night? Your name is in the story that broke. That means their competition is one step ahead of them, here on the scene."

"This kind of story, the shooting of a cop, the rape of a girl, is everyday stuff to the big news people," Peter said. "Why so much interest in this?" He knew the answer but he wanted Smith to say it.

Smith began to count off on his fingers. "There's Cyrus Steele, Fred Knowlton, Roger Littlejohn, Henry Kobler, David Byrnes, and on and on. Some of the biggest fortunes in America live here in Wynwood. Oil, steel, automobiles, computers—big business in spades. If any one of them or any of their families are involved, it's a big story. To ignore that possibility would risk being scooped and laughed at by the competition. So they're going to make a story out of this whether there is one or not."

"Do you think there can be a connection between one of these rich families and what's happened?"

Smith shrugged. "I've already suggested to you what I think about today's adolescents—from ten to thirty," he said. "There's three or four dozen of that kind of adolescent in town. Nothing has to be too far out for someone in that group. It could be."

"Mr. Styles is different," Ben Gleason said. "From the other reporters, I mean. He wasn't here for a story. A girl in trouble came to him and he tried to help."

"I know," Smith said, "which is why I'm listening."

"That girl's whole life depends a lot on how she comes out of this mess," Peter said. "As far as covering it professionally goes, Smith, I'm not a day-to-day crime reporter. Whatever I may have to write about, it will come after the whole thing is wrapped up and I can make some kind of sensible statement about it."

"How can we help?" Smith asked.

"Ben has asked if he could work with me. He'd be invaluable. There's a whole segment of the town you haven't mentioned—the local people, the shopkeepers, the restaurant and bar owners, the plumbers and electricians and carpenters, the people who do the work and supply the services not covered by Wilson's Maxi-Service. The local kids; are they as irresponsible as those old adolescents on the other side of the tracks you've mentioned?"

"If Ben wants to team up with you it's all right with me," Smith said. He smiled. "If he writes a piece for us that raises hell, we can blame it on you."

"Be my guest," Peter said. "About local kids?"

"They're different from the kids on the other side of the tracks, to use your phrase," Smith said. "Most of them don't go beyond high school. Then they go to work. There's plenty of work in Wynwood. The rich don't want to do anything for themselves. The rich kids all go to college, then they hang around waiting for a relative to die so they'll never have to do anything!"

"That's probably an exaggeration," Peter said. "And surely some of the locals go to college. I was told Mike Quinlan and Dick Robbins played football somewhere."

"I'd say half the locals either go right on to college from

high school or have a go at it later, like me," Ben Gleason said. "Most of them wind up here, doing service jobs in the town. There's always work here, which isn't true out in the rest of the world."

"You don't need a college degree to install some plumbing," Smith said. "You learn by doing." He rubbed the bowl of his pipe along the side of his nose and then polished it in the palm of his hand. "I've had some thoughts that aren't based on any facts at all. Judith Larsen is local. If she was rich, I'd guess it was one of the local boys who tried to rape her. Since she's local, I'm tempted to think one of the rich kids went after her."

"There's a feud between the locals and the rich?" Peter asked.

"The young ones, I think, have a kind of mutual contempt for each other," Smith said. "What do you think, Ben?"

Gleason looked uncomfortable. "I guess it's a kind of envy," he said. "I had to work my way through State. Most of us who went on to college had to make it the hard way. It kind of gets you to watch someone like Billy Steele, out there in his sailboat, not having to do anything at all except enjoy himself. But raping the other guys' women? That would have to be just some individual freak." He shook his head. "It's not a way of life for most of us."

"So what's your next move, Mr. Styles?" Smith asked.

"Ear to the ground, I guess," Peter said. "Try to hear what the local music sounds like. I'd like to talk to Dr. Kreuger before I go much further."

"Perhaps I should warn you, Kreuger is a kind of prize bastard," Smith said. "Good doctor, but a louse!"

Yesterday the town of Wynwood had had a bland, relaxed feeling to it, with its well-kept lawns and gardens, its lake, its views of the distant Berkshire hills, its people dressed in casual but expensive summer clothes. There had been a kind of peace and order, paid for and expected. The only ripple on the smooth surface of this community had occurred some six months ago when a trooper on routine patrol had been shot down, presumably by some escaping criminal who just happened to be passing through in the middle of the night. The locals had been mildly disturbed that the outside world of crime and violence could have invaded their territory even for the time it took to shoot down a trooper and speed away. Today everyone had to stop short and look around apprehensively. An "outsider," Peter Styles, well-known name to many of them, had forced them to face the ugly fact that the murderer of Dick Robbins had taken a potshot at the disturbed girl. She had apparently been wandering around in the woods at night when she should have been home in bed, or at least watching a late movie on television.

"Listening to people, you'd think, somehow, Judith was responsible for bringing the killer to the surface," Ben Gleason told Peter.

They were headed for the hospital on the outskirts of town where Dr. Kreuger's psychiatric clinic was located. Gleason had taken a note Peter had left at the *Advocate* for his friend Frank Devery, enclosing his door key so that Devery could go to the camp and wait for him. *Advocate* workers had reported to him that in addition to calls from news services and reporters they'd been flooded by calls from Wynwood residents asking for information. If there was a killer on the loose in town, people felt they had a right to know.

"I suppose they think if I hadn't found the bullet they'd be safe," Peter said.

"Something like that. Tell me, Peter—may I call you that?"

"Of course."

"What do you expect to get from Dr. Kreuger?"

"Help, if he'll give it," Peter said. "Judith was in his care for weeks after the rape attempt. And I don't know why I say 'attempt.' In a clinical sense she wasn't 'penetrated'; but she was mauled, abused, violated. That's rape, not attempted rape. Kreuger listened to her story over and over, if I understand the technique. He came to the conclusion that it had never really happened, that she'd put on some kind of self-deluding charade, stripped herself naked, thrown herself around on the ground, discarded her clothes in the stream. But it turns out he was wrong. She was telling him the truth. Now I want to hear again what she told him. I want to hear her description of the rapist, every minute detail, everything Kreuger discarded when he decided she was a mental case. The townspeople are right, you know. This character is wandering around town, probably gossiping with them at the post office, in the local bars. Kreuger may have the very best lead if we can get to him."

"But Judith would tell you all that, wouldn't she, Peter?"

"For six weeks everyone's been telling her she had a nightmare," Peter said. "She must have begun to doubt herself from time to time. She's forced herself to dull her memory about the man. What she told Kreuger in the first days was hot off the griddle. He must have made notes, maybe even kept tapes of their sessions. What Judith told him then, hours after it happened, a day or two after, could give us a picture we haven't got and that she can no longer force herself to recall."

"Kreuger isn't going to like you for proving his diagnosis has been wrong all these weeks," Gleason said.

"He's not God," Peter said. "Judith was so hysterical it could have been an easy mistake to make. I'm not questioning his competence. I just want the information he's got. He doesn't seem to be popular from what your Mr.

Smith told me; and Judith says she overheard Kay Logan, her mother's nurse, telling George Wilson that Kreuger is a womanizer, after all the nurses at the hospital."

Gleason grinned. "They say he has 'em lined up like cordwood for whenever he feels the itch. I guess he's popular enough with a lot of them."

The hospital was an attractive gray stone building, ivy covering the walls facing the street. The grounds around it were expertly landscaped, probably cared for, Peter thought, by George Wilson's crew.

The psychiatric clinic was in a sort of annex building at the rear, connected to the main building by a covered walkway. They went into what was a small reception room. The receptionist, a pretty young girl in a starched white uniform, greeted Ben Gleason with a prim smile.

"Good morning, Miss Lewis," Ben said.

"My name is Peter Styles. I'd like to talk to Dr. Kreuger," Peter said.

"You have an appointment?" The girl was looking down at a log book on her desk.

"No, but I—"

"Have you consulted with Dr. Kreuger before?"

"I'm not a patient. I—"

"Dr. Kreuger can see you on the twenty-seventh at three P.M.," Miss Lewis said.

"That's three weeks away," Peter said.

"Unless it's an emergency," the girl said.

"I think you could call it that," Peter said.

A little red light on the phone at the girl's elbow blinked. Miss Lewis excused herself and picked up the phone. "Yes, Nora?" She looked surprised. "Well, sure. Yes, I'll send him right in." She put down the phone. "It seems Dr. Kreuger is willing to see you now, Mr. Styles."

Peter noticed the intercom box on the girl's desk. It had obviously been open to someone on the inside. Nora could be Mike Quinlan's wife, he thought. He was directed through a door at the far end of the room. Gleason was informed that he was not included in the green light.

At the end of a short corridor Nora Quinlan was waiting for Peter. She smiled at him. "Magic," she said. "The intercom system was open. I make decisions for Ada Lewis. Dr. Kreuger has been expecting you."

"That's a surprise."

"He's a psychiatrist, Mr. Styles. He knows how people's minds work. As soon as the news was out this morning he said you'd be in. If you'll wait here a moment I'll let him know you're here."

She left him alone and went down the corridor to a door at the end. A moment later she appeared and beckoned to him. Beyond the door a very good-looking man in his late forties sat at a desk. He was tall, blond, with bright, inquisitive blue eyes. There was nothing medical about his appearance. He had on a pale blue linen sports jacket, a white Brooks Brothers button-down shirt with a military striped tie, gray slacks, black-and-white sport shoes. A just-on-the-way-to-the-country-club look, Peter thought. Perhaps a psychiatrist dealing with disturbed people would want to avoid the medical look.

"I've been expecting you, Mr. Styles," the doctor said. It was a pleasant, almost musical voice. This was a charm boy, Peter thought. No wonder the ladies were lined up "like cordwood" waiting for a nod from this matinee idol.

"It's good of you to see me during your working hours," Peter said. "I gather from your receptionist that I should have had to stand in line for three weeks. How did I get so lucky?"

"Curiosity," Kreuger said. "Of course I know your work in *Newsview;* but as of today you're suddenly involved in a case of mine. It's not difficult to project how a first-rate mind will work. It's the sick ones that are tricky. You discovered this morning that what Judith Larsen told you happened last night was probably true. You found a bullet in a tree that confirmed her story of being shot at. The interesting offshoot is that the gun used to fire the shot appears to be the one used to murder a state trooper here six months ago. News does get around fast in a small town."

"So what made you think I'd turn up here to see you?"

"Because you had obviously fallen into a trap, Mr. Styles." Kreuger had picked up a gold pencil on his desk and was tapping it gently on a pad in front of him. "The bullet in the tree proved to you and almost everyone else in this town that Judith not only told the truth about last night but about the so-called rape attempt six weeks ago. That being proved—to your satisfaction—you would obviously come here to find out from me what she told me about that rapist six weeks ago, when it had just happened."

"On the nose, Doctor," Peter said.

"My source," Kreuger said, "is Nora Quinlan, who gets it from the horse's mouth, who is her husband and in on the case. Judith now says the man last night was not the rapist—a smaller more agile man. Right?"

"Which suggests a group or gang," Peter said.

"Not to me," Dr. Kreuger said. "I have an advantage over you, Mr. Styles, because Judith has been my patient for weeks."

"Which, as you guessed, is why I'm here."

"You won't like it, Mr. Styles. You won't like it at all. Let's go over it. The bullet you found in the tree proves what? That a shot was fired, if not last night at least very recently, from a gun that was used six months ago to murder Trooper Robbins. Does that substantiate the rest of Judith's story—a man in a ski mask, swearing at her, running down the parallel road after her, firing at her when she tripped and fell? You only have her word for that part of it. And her word is the word of a sick, disturbed girl who made up a whole story about a rape six weeks ago."

"You don't think that the bullet proves that she has always been telling the truth?"

"Not for a minute," Kreuger said. "I've listened to it, over and over. There never was a rape—or a powerful man who threw her around. A sick invention. This girl had too much to bear in the past; the violent death of her father, the tragic accident that has immobilized her mother, the murder of her fiancé. It's tilted her out of the world of sanity. I've seen this kind of thing hundreds of times. Suddenly the victim can't live without being the object of violence and pain. If it doesn't happen to them automatically, they have to invent it. That's what happened to Judith six weeks ago. She had to attract attention to herself with a new attack. Quite a picture, isn't it? A girl out there in the woods all alone, tearing off her clothes, hurling herself on the ground and into a clump of brambles, beating and clawing at herself, and then running naked out into the road, flagging down a patrol car she probably knew was due to pass about that time. That girl flipped her wig, but totally, Mr. Styles."

Peter sat very still, feeling his muscles grow tense. "And last night, you say, was another invention?"

Dr. Krueger's bright eyes narrowed. "There's an outside chance that it wasn't," he said. "Just a chance that it really did happen. You know, that rape story six weeks ago was handled with some compassion and consideration by people who knew about it. Dr. Smalley, her stepfather, we here at the clinic, the troopers who investigated, the local newspaper—we kept the story to ourselves, or tried to." He shrugged. "A trooper talks to his girl, his wife. Some smartass at the newspaper passes it on to a friend—in confidence. It leaks. A lot of people got to know about a dreamed-up giant in a ski mask. Somebody thought they'd have some fun with the foolish girl who kept going, after dark, to the same place in spite of what she said had happened there. You notice there was no real attack. He ran down a parallel road, shouting at her—the easy way, where he could see where he was going."

"And then fired a shot at her with the weapon he'd used to murder Dick Robbins?" Peter asked.

"I haven't said there isn't a homicidal nut loose here in town," Dr. Kreuger said. "I'm just telling you the rape story was a sick invention. I can't give you any information about a giant mauler because he never existed. Last night could be real, but one has to wonder."

Peter stood up. "Have you ever been asked to leave town, Doctor?" he asked.

Dr. Kreuger's smile suggested wry amusement. "A husband or two have suggested it might be good for my health," he said. "Practicing medicine here in Wynwood is too profitable to let a pleasant affair get in the way of it."

"I've been asked," Peter said. He described what had happened at the camp to his typewriter, his notes, his clothes and personal equipment. "Right down to my toothbrush, Doctor, and a note taped to the mantel in the living room and scrawled on the mirror in the bathroom suggesting I get out of town and mind my own business. You read sick minds so well—what does that suggest to you?"

"Vandalism is one of today's number one sports," Kreuger said.

"It suggests to me," Peter said, "that I'm close to some kind of truth that must be kept hidden at all costs. That bullet in the tree suggests that someone has the means to silence me completely if I don't go quietly."

"And are you flirting with some truth you haven't mentioned to me, Mr. Styles?"

"So far only the personal conviction that Judith Larsen is as sane as I am; that everything she's told you, the police, and her family is the truth."

"That she has been attacked on two different occasions by two different men—wearing the same ski mask in mid-August? In a court of law I'd have to be the expert witness testifying against that theory, Mr. Styles. I don't believe it for a moment."

"So who am I threatening, and with what?" Peter asked.

2

That was, to coin a cliché, the $64,000 question. Dr. Kreuger did not offer an answer to it.

"Nor do I have a clue to the answer," Peter told his friend Frank Devery.

Frank Devery could have been the role model for the TV editor Lou Grant: square, solid, balding, tough, yet, Peter knew from his own grim experiences, a man of boundless compassion. Devery was at the camp, waiting, when Peter finally got there.

"I brought your clothes," Devery said to Peter. "On the way up I wondered if I should have brought you a bulletproof vest."

Peter had stopped in town and bought himself a new coffee machine, and it was brewing. "It's nice to see a friendly face," he said, as he prepared crockery mugs for the pouring.

"I didn't come here to hold your hand," Devery said. "You know who owns a controlling block of stock in *Newsview*? Fred Knowlton of National Communications. He has a house on the main drag here somewhere. This is his town."

"You have to ask him if it's all right for *Newsview* to cover the story?"

"I should give you the back of my hand for that one," Devery said. "You know damn well I wouldn't work for anyone for five minutes who told me what I can and cannot cover and put into print."

"I know. Just teasing," Peter said. "But you play it cozy?"

"I know you," Devery said. "You need nursemaiding. You came up here to write a novel and here you are, back on the old rails again, chasing after some violence. I'd like to see you wrap it up in a hurry and get back to what you set out to do. Fred Knowlton's father was one of the first rich settlers to come here to Wynwood. Fred grew up here, knows the place like the back of his hands, loves it. If anyone knows this town, can bring pressure to bear if it's needed, Fred's the man. He and I have been friends a long time. I thought he could be useful to you."

The signal light on the coffee machine indicated that the brewing process was done. Peter poured two mugs of coffee.

"I've gotten myself in trouble," he said, "by being unreasonably stubborn. For some reason I've let myself be persuaded that this girl, Judith Larsen, is as sane as you are and is telling me the exact truth. That goes against her doctor, her psychiatrist, her family, and the state police."

"So, you're probably wrong," Devery said.

"I've been working for you for seventeen years, Frank. How often have you known me to go out on a limb for someone and be wrong about it?"

"I've doubted you often," Devery said. "So far you're batting a thousand. But everyone gets to be wrong sometime."

"Talk to her with me, will you, Frank? Make some kind of judgment of your own."

Devery sipped his coffee, frowning. "We could rephrase the question you asked earlier," he said. "Why should your believing this girl make you a threat to someone, make them want to drive you away? The overly simply answer is that you're opening up two old cases that have been dropped, a murder and a rape. Oh, I suppose the police never drop a case when one of their own has been killed, but they'd obviously run out of leads until you found that bullet. The rape case was dead, written off by family, a trusted medical man, a famous psychiatrist, and the police. Now you, a man with a national reputation as an investigative reporter, start trying to persuade people that those judgments, by trusted people, are all wet. You're trying to revive a dead issue that someone wants to have stay dead. You need something beside the girl, Peter, to back you up, because I gather the people of this town has made up their minds about her."

"Talk to her with me before we do anything else," Peter said. "See what you think."

Devery took the last swallow of his coffee. "So what are we waiting for?" he said.

It was after the normal lunch hour when the two friends drove along the village green, turned off on the side street that led to the Maxi-Service yard and the driveway up to George Wilson's house. The parked cars of Wilson's workmen were still scattered around the Maxi-Service barns and sheds, but the men themselves were evidently all off on jobs somewhere. There were no cars outside Wilson's when they got there, but from somewhere—possibly the rear terrace, Peter thought—came the sound of a radio or a record player. Someone who liked modern rock music had it on loud.

The brass knocker on the front door produced no results, nor the electric doorbell to one side.

"Music sounds as if it was coming from the terrace at the back," Peter said. "Let's have a look."

"If that's your young woman's taste in music I may be prejudiced before I get to talk to her," Devery said. "What's that gag I heard the other day? Instead of the young lovers saying 'they're playing our song,' they say 'they're playing our noise.' "

The music evidently blotted out the sound of the men's footsteps on the flagstone terrace as they rounded the corner of the house. Rose Wilson sat in her wheelchair under the shade of an awning, staring out at the valley beyond, not seeing what was there. Out on the grass, in the bright sun, the ample Kay Logan was stretched out on a blanket, blond hair spread out around her, breasts bared for a good suntanning. She gave a startled cry as she caught sight of Peter and Devery, scrambled to her feet, covering herself with the blanket that she snatched up from the grass.

"Don't you characters ever knock before you invade a lady's boudoir?" she said. She laughed, as though being exposed hadn't really displeased her.

"This is Frank Devery, the editor of my magazine," Peter said. "Kay Logan. I'm sorry, Miss Logan. We tried rousing someone at the front door. No one answered, but we could hear the music."

It came from a cassette player resting on a wicker table beside Rose Wilson's wheelchair. It was so deafeningly loud Peter had to raise his voice to be heard. Kay Logan went over and turned it off. She managed, her back turned, to button up the front of her blouse. Big, capable hands worked at putting her hair in order. She turned and looked down at her patient.

"She doesn't hear—or care, if she does," she said, as if that needed explaining.

"I'm looking for Judith," Peter said.

"I don't suppose I could have expected two handsome gents to be calling on me," Kay Logan said. "I don't know where Judith is. She took off."

"Took off?"

"Stadler and his boys stayed here for quite a while after you left, Mr. Styles. Cops have more senseless questions to ask than a jealous husband. After they'd gone, Judith checked out with mama here, and took off."

"Checked out?"

"She always tells the madam if she's going somewhere,

down to the village, or to the library, or to see the doctor, or just for a walk. Not that it makes any difference what she tells her. She could tell her she was going on a slow boat to China. It doesn't register. Hear no evil, speak no evil, see no evil! God help her, she's a nothing."

"Yours must be a rough job, unable to communicate with your patient," Devery said.

"It has its good points," Kay Logan said. "I don't get any complaints like you do from most invalids."

"Where did Judith tell her mother she was going this time?" Peter asked.

"I don't know. I guess I'd gone into the kitchen for something. I'm just guessing that she told her mother where she was going. She always does."

"You saw her go?"

"She was headed down toward the village."

"Walking or in a car?"

"She's got a little Honda she drives around," Kay Logan said.

Devery gave the big blond woman a surprisingly warm smile. "I'm like the jealous husband, Miss Logan, full of questions. How long have you been on this job?"

"About two and a half years. The lady had her accident a little more than three years ago. Surgery here, then the Mayo Clinic, a half dozen specialists after that. Nothing anyone could do for her. She wouldn't stop breathing, but she couldn't live either. My God, if anything like that ever happened to me I'd want them to pull the plug." For a moment the woman's face showed something like pity. "I think if she could she'd ask me to hold the pillow down over her face some night."

"Her husband could have left her hospitalized," Devery said.

"You paid any hospital bills lately, mister? Anyway, George isn't that kind of a guy. This was her home; she'd always loved it, loved the countryside. Here there are no tubes, or jerks in white uniforms pushing and shoving her around, not giving a damn."

"So you came on the job when Wilson moved his wife back home?" Devery said.

Kay Logan nodded. "I thought it would be a short haul, but here I am."

"So you were here when some of the worst things happened to Judith," Devery said. "Her fiancé murdered, the rape business?"

"The worst thing that happened to her was before my time," Kay Logan said, nodding toward the figure in the wheelchair. "That anchored her here where I guess she didn't want to be. She never got over George taking her father's place. It doesn't make sense because the madam here was a real happy woman until she did a swan dive down the cellar stairs."

"That was real," Devery said, "and the murder of her boyfriend was real. You go along with everyone else that the rape thing never really happened? That she invented it?"

Her smile was thin and bitter. "You're not a woman, mister. No woman ever hears about a rape attempt without thinking 'it could be.' Read your newspaper and every day you'll see an account of some freak breaking into a city apartment and raping and sodomizing some seventy-five-year-old. You don't have to be a sexy doll, just a woman! Yes, when Judith came up with her story I thought 'it could be.' She's attractive, she's young, she had no guy hanging around to protect her. Anyone who had an eye on her would know that she went down to that property of hers, night after night, all by herself. Yes, I thought 'it could be.' But then it turned out she wasn't really raped in a physical sense, just a roughing up, if it happened at all. A good country doctor didn't believe it happened. A psychiatrist, who knows all about eating women alive, didn't believe it happened. The cops couldn't find any evidence."

"So you stopped thinking 'it could be'?"

"There's one more thing that made up my mind," Kay Logan said. "Let's say for a moment it did happen—a crazy man in a ski mask tearing off her clothes, all that. Would any person in their right mind go back to the place where it happened time after time, night after night, with no way to protect herself? Either it happened and she wanted it to happen again, or it never happened so she had no reason to be afraid."

"But it did happen, or started to happen again last night," Peter said.

"She says."

"The bullet. The bullet was there. I found it."

"You'll find an explanation for that, I imagine, before you're through, Mr. Styles. Everybody says you're tops at finding explanations for things."

End of the line again, Peter thought. "If I don't catch up with Judith in town will you tell her I very much want to see her, talk to her?" he asked.

"You should know that George Wilson doesn't want you messing around with this," Kay Logan said.

"Keep your ear to the ground, Miss Logan, and you'll hear why there's no way I can back off now."

On a lazy, warm summer afternoon Wynwood's village green wasn't Times Square in the rush hour. Peter stopped at the *Advocate* office, hoping to catch up with Ben Gleason or even Brad Smith, the editor. Young Gleason could circulate and very quickly find out who had seen Judith and where. Both men were out of the office, Brad Smith due back about four, Ben Gleason's schedule unknown. The *Advocate,* a weekly, didn't go to press for another few days. No one apparently kept very strict hours until the deadline approached. A helpful secretary suggested that on a beautiful Thursday afternoon you'd be most likely to find any citizen of Wynwood either on the golf course, the tennis courts, the lake—swimming or boating—or just sunbathing in their own backyards. Barring all those possibilities there was a coffee shop in the shopping center where people popped in and out. Peter left word for Ben Gleason to get in touch and that he should be back at the Jordan's camp in an hour or so.

Frank Devery had used the time while Peter was talking to the secretary to call his friend Fred Knowlton on a pay phone in the corner of the office. He found Knowlton at home, was welcomed and given directions to the Knowlton estate.

Estate was the proper word for the Knowlton property. There was a mile of blue stone driveway through perfectly tended pine and birch woods to what looked like a medieval stone castle on the top of a hill, surrounded by magnificent old maples and oaks. The lawns, the flower beds, the hedges and shrubs were cared for by experts. Somehow Peter expected to be greeted by footmen and butlers. Instead, a good-looking older man with silver-white hair and dark black eyebrows waited for them at the front door. Fred Knowlton was wearing casual tan slacks, navy blue sneakers, a white shirt open at the neck, sleeves rolled up. His smile was relaxed, his dark eyes bright with pleasure as he greeted Devery.

"Tried to get you up here often for a weekend, Frank. Suddenly you just appear. Unpredictable is the word for you." He turned to Peter and held out his hand. "I've waited too long for this, Peter Styles. I've always been secretly proud to have a connection with a publication that boasts of having your by-line."

He suggested they talk in the "game room." The afternoon sun was a little too glaring at this time of day. The game room was equipped with a billiard table, glassed-in gun racks with a collection of hunting rifles and shotguns, a trophy case containing silver mugs, cups, and platters that Knowlton had obviously won at some sport.

"Fred was a scratch golfer not too long ago," Devery explained.

"When you pass sixty the going gets a little tougher," Knowlton said. "I play from a six handicap these days."

"I'll remember to wait another ten years to take you on," Peter said.

They sat in comfortable leather armchairs around a green baize-topped poker table, cards and chips at the ready in case anyone felt so inclined. The sun, Knowlton said, was not yet over the yardarm as far as he was concerned, but on this special occasion would anyone like a drink?

"Maybe after Peter's had a chance to talk to you," Devery said.

"I only heard this morning that you were in town, Peter," Knowlton said. "One of the reasons you found me at home instead of out on the golf course was that I thought I might hear from you."

"You're the second man today who expected me to appear," Peter said.

"The other?"

"Dr. Kreuger at the psychiatric clinic."

Knowlton grinned. "About the Larsen girl, not yourself I hope."

"Peter finds himself on the other side of a general bias about Judith Larsen, Fred," Devery said. "He needs to talk to someone who really knows this town and its people."

"I was four years old when my father built this house," Knowlton said. "I should know something about Wynwood after sixty years. I grew up here. This was my base when I went to prep school and college. I guess I've spent every summer of my life here. We traveled in the winters. My father didn't like New England winters. You stirred up a storm, Peter, it would seem. Stadler must have been shocked, when you found that bullet, to know that the man who murdered one of his troopers was still right here in town after six months."

"All we know for certain is that the gun is still here," Peter said. "It wasn't necessarily fired this second time by the same man."

Knowlton nodded. "I'd thought of that," he said. "I should have known you wouldn't take anything for granted."

Peter told Knowlton about the vandalism at the camp and the message suggesting he leave town. "I have to conclude that I'm close to something, but the trouble is I haven't the faintest idea what it is. What can you tell me about the murder of Dick Robbins, Mr. Knowlton? Stadler and his troopers don't want to talk. They've missed the boat somewhere."

Knowlton's face clouded. "That came a lot closer to me than just the shooting of a cop on duty," he said. "Long ago my father started something in this town that I've carried on after him. We were the first of the wealthy families to buy and build in this area. Wynwood was just a small, country village, a few dairy farms and a limestone quarry. Kids grew up here and went away as quickly as they could because there wasn't anything here for them. To cut it short, my father was interested in the local people. The workmen who built the house came from here. When my old man saw bright kids in the families of those workmen he became a sort of patron to them. I can't tell you how many kids he helped put through college, technical school, medical school, law school. And as my father persuaded some of his wealthy friends to buy here, build, and settle, they followed his pattern. I don't suppose there's a small town anywhere where so many young people have been given a lift up. In my time one of the kids I undertook to help was Dick Robbins."

"So you knew him well," Peter said.

Knowlton nodded. "He was one of many, but he was a special one—*the* one." The cloud darkened. "Forty years ago my wife died in childbirth, Peter. Our baby, too. I never remarried. That's as close as I ever came to a family. Young Dick was being brought up by a foster family here in town. His father ran out when he was a baby. His mother became an alcoholic. She hired out as a housemaid to some of the rich families, but she couldn't hold a job because of the booze. Then cancer of the liver and she was gone when Dick was about ten. The family that took him in were some kind of distant cousins, no money, kids of their own. One of the teachers in the local elementary school called my attention to Dick. He was bright, had a future, but no base to work from. I took an interest, and somehow the boy and I hit it off. He came and went here as though he were a member of my family. I got him through high school, and then college. He was a star athlete and a damn good student. He—he was like a son to me, Peter."

Peter waited for him to go on.

"Then there was law school. He saw the law as a way to improve the society we live in."

"But instead he became a state trooper?" Devery asked.

"That was intended to be just a stopgap, a practical experience in enforcing the law he felt he needed. As a matter of fact, that night he was killed was intended to be his last night as a trooper. They said he was going on leave to get married, but he intended to resign, marry, and go into law practice for himself. I was prepared to help him until he got going."

"Help him and Judith?" Peter asked. "You must know her."

"Of course. As a matter of fact Dick met her here, in this house."

"You knew her that well?"

"No, I didn't know her at all when they met. Every New Year's I give a party here. Everyone in town is invited, and I'm proud to say almost everyone comes. Food, eggnog, happy New Year! She came—just somebody in town. She met Dick and it went off like a Roman candle."

"You approved?" Peter asked.

"I wasn't an old grandmother, sitting around suggesting that no one was good enough for my golden boy," Knowlton said. "But—" He hesitated. "What you're involved with, Peter, centers on Judith. I don't want anything I say to affect your thinking about her."

"Peter's got a hunch about her," Devery said. "That's about as easy to move around as the Rock of Gibraltar."

"She was five years younger than Dick when they met," Knowlton said. "She seemed a little immature to me at first, withdrawn, terribly shy. Then, gradually, through Dick, I got to know her story—her father, her mother. I got the impression she wasn't happy with her home situation, had always resented George Wilson, her stepfather. I thought she saw Dick as a glamorous way to escape all that. I didn't want him to be used. You can pick up enough problems of your own along the way without having to carry someone else's load of iron. I suppose she sensed I wasn't running up the flags when they decided to marry. I'm a hunch man, too, Peter. I was afraid it wasn't going to work, but I didn't get into the act except for one time." He shook his head, smiling. "Dick and I were having a nightcap in this room one night. I suggested to him that he didn't have to shoulder responsibilities before he was ready in order to get into the hay with the lady. I even told him this was a big house and he could be as private here as he wanted. You know what he told me? They weren't having sex! In this day and age! He told me she was old-fashioned about it, wanted to wait till it was certainly forever. That's why he was in such a hurry. He had it real bad for her."

"Didn't that make you feel better about her?"

"I'm not sure," Knowlton said. "I'm not sure I believed any girl today could get to be twenty years old without being had somewhere along the way. I'm not sure I didn't think she was using a phony chastity to get Dick locked in before he needed to be."

"So you didn't and don't like her?" Peter asked.

"That's going a little far," Knowlton said. "She was pleasant, polite, not too much humor, but she could carry on an intelligent conversation about a variety of things. I even felt some pity for her, locked away with a stepfather she didn't like and a mother who was suddenly a nothing, a zero. But I loved Dick. I wanted things to be right for him."

"But what happened to him had nothing whatever to do with Judith," Peter said.

"Not really," Knowlton said. A little nerve twitched high up on his tanned cheek. "He would have been married the next day and in bed with the lady he wanted so badly. Maybe he was a little careless. Maybe his mind wasn't all in one place, where it should have been."

"From what I've heard he followed all the routines," Peter said. "Started to follow a suspicious car, reported it to the barracks on his car radio—make of car, license-plate numbers, the route they were following. Nothing absent-minded about that, was there?"

"No, he was a good cop. He was good at everything he did—good student, good athlete. He'd certainly have been a good husband and one hell of a lawyer once he got started."

"So where did he get absentminded?"

"I don't know—the last minute. The last words he spoke on his car radio were that he'd got his suspect pulled over and 'I'm leaving my car to arrest the sonofabitch.' If he spoke to his killer we have no record of it. He was angry because this chase had kept him beyond his normal quitting time. The next day was to have been D-day, his big day, the day when he acquired a lady for life. He was angry and that could have made him careless."

"Did he shut off the car radio when he left it?"

"No." Again the little nerve twitched. "The radio trooper at the barracks heard the shots, four of them. They found three of them in Dick's head. They never found the fourth slug, although they searched for a month."

"Maybe Robbins fired it and it hit the car the killer escaped in," Peter suggested.

"Dick's gun was in his hand, but it hadn't been fired," Knowlton said.

"Were you satisfied with the efforts Stadler and his men made to try to find the killer?" Peter asked.

"When you've lost someone who's dear to you you're never satisfied," Knowlton said. "But—yes. Dick was one of them. Cops don't like cop killers. But they had so damn little to go on. There was the license plate on the car. It turned out to have been stolen off someone's Volkswagen across the state. No way to trace the car itself. They checked out a hundred or more black and dark blue Lincoln-Mercurys in a tristate area. Nothing turned up."

"What started Robbins after that car in the first place? Speeding?"

"No. In this town, Peter, there are eleven large houses—estates—like mine. In them are works of art—paintings, sculpture, silver, jewelry—that must run into millions of dollars. We all have some form of protection—burglar alarms, people living in. Maxi-Service provides a private patrol system if we choose to hire them. If someone goes away on a trip and leaves a house unoccupied, the state police are notified and their regular patrols keep a special eye out. That's what happened with Dick. The Henry Kobler place was empty, family in Europe, servants given a vacation. Maxi-Service was covering and the state police had been alerted. Dick's patrol route took him past the Kobler place. As he was approaching, this black Lincoln-Mercury came out the Koblers' front gate. When the driver spotted the patrol car with its roof lights he took off at high speed. He ignored Dick's siren. Dick reported back to the barracks on his radio. It could be a robbery, someone should check out the Kobler house, he'd get the man in the car. The rest I've told you. Dick didn't make it."

"Had the Kobler house been robbed?"

"No. Nothing taken, no sign of a break-in. What the guy was doing there nobody knows. Stadler picked up some tire marks, photographed them, made a mold of one of them. They never led anywhere."

"You said Maxi-Service had been hired to protect the Kobler place."

"They don't mount a guard," Knowlton said. "They patrol, like the cops, except they go right into the property and look around. They'd been to the Kobler place about an hour before Dick saw the car coming out the front gates. They saw nothing when they were there. They would, normally, have covered the place once more in the early hours of the morning. By then there were cops everywhere. Incidentally, I offered a reward of fifty thousand dollars to anyone who came up with evidence that would lead to the arrest and conviction of Dick's killer. It still stands, in case you get lucky, Peter."

"All this protection," Peter said. "Burglar alarms, Maxi-Service, the state police—and I take it servants, gardeners, the like. You people with big estates feel threatened by the locals, or some segment of them?"

Knowlton gave Peter a grim little smile. "This place became a public fishbowl a few years back," he said. "Cyrus Steele bought property and built here about ten years ago. I guess he was a little too proud of what he had here and he opened up to the press for a big housewarming. Not just the local press, but national magazines, newspapers, radio, and TV. Suddenly the whole damn world knew that Wynwood might be the richest town in America, with priceless art objects, jewelry, fabulous automobiles, television sets, jewelry—all just here for the taking! It was like an invitation to big-time thieves all over the whole damn world. Ever since then, let a stranger appear in town and he could be some kind of international operator here to steal the gold fillings out of our teeth."

"And have you been invaded by thieves?"

"Not successfully, not on a big scale," Knowlton said. His smile relaxed. "I seem to remember your doing a piece for *Newsview* on gun control, attacking the National Rifle Association. Don't try to sell gun control in Wynwood, Peter. Everyone over ten years old in this town who can handle a gun owns one. Would you believe the Women's Club in this town has a rifle range where all the members, young and old, practice once a week? That word has gotten out too, and the small-time crooks aren't eager to risk getting shot between the eyes. There's been some petty stuff taken, like tools, a couple of cars, small stuff that could have been carried out in a coat pocket by a disloyal servant or delivery boy. Or even a house guest. What the cops call 'souvenir snatching.' Did you know that guests steal the White House blind? They take a butter knife, a sauce dish, an embroidered napkin—just for souvenirs."

"I've got a collection of hotel bath towels at home," Devery said.

Knowlton suggested that the time had come for that drink. Devery would have Scotch on the rocks. Peter passed. He was not close to the moment of relaxing. Appearing, as if by magic, was a houseman wearing a white coat. He took the drink order and went away. There must be a signal button somewhere Peter hadn't noticed.

"Tell me, Mr. Knowlton," he said. "You know the town, you've helped local kids; Dick Robbins was one of them. How recently were you involved with him?"

"Like yesterday," Knowlton said. "I mean, this goes back to when I took over from my father, inherited this house—and a hell of a lot of money, I might add. But most immediately, Dick was twenty-six years old when he died. He came into my life when he was ten. Particularly, in the last five years, I've been pretty close to the local scene, especially to Dick. He grew up here, went to school and college with his own generation, knew the younger kids in those families who were coming along. I have three kids I'm helping right now—on Dick's advice."

"You haven't been turned off by the picture we get of kids today—drugs, liquor, sex? With what drugs and liquor cost, you have to add crime. That doesn't turn you off?"

Knowlton nodded. "It would turn me off if I saw it all around me," he said. "I remember wondering, long ago, if my father was as kind and generous as he let everyone think he was. He was pretty tough with me. I wondered if he was just protecting himself and his property by helping local kids. Maybe that's what I've been doing since I took over from him. I don't think so, but I suppose there could be a touch of it." He laughed. "A little like the 'trickle-down' economy we hear about in Washington these days—the rich letting something trickle down to the poor and underprivileged."

"I think it was Hubert Humphrey who had the best description of that trickle-down theory," Devery said. "He said it was like feeding your cattle extra grain so, when it passed through them, there'd be something special for the sparrows to eat." He and Knowlton enjoyed the joke. They were drifting, Peter thought.

"So you have contact with local young people," he said, with a touch of impatience. "Dick Robbins's generation and the kids that came after him. How do the kids in Wynwood raise hell?"

"If I knew why you were asking these questions, Peter—"

"I'm still with Judith Larsen and what happened to her," Peter said. "I don't really give a damn about your town, Mr. Knowlton. I never knew your boy, Dick Robbins. I regret, because of you and because of Judith—and because of society in general—what happened to him. But Judith burst into my life last night, asking for help. I believe what she told me. The best way I can help her is to convince other people she's telling the truth. If I succeed in that, then others will join me in seeing to it that nothing more happens to her. If she's being victimized by some hopped-up kids, locals or rich kids, I mean to stop it."

"You're a nice man, Peter," Knowlton said.

"He's a nice man who's being threatened if he doesn't leave your town, Fred," Devery said. "Whoever is gunning for the girl is letting him know he's a target, too."

Knowlton didn't speak until the man in the white coat had brought a drink for him, one for Devery, and a glass of iced tea garnished with mint for Peter, "just in case, sir."

"There aren't any gangs of kids or young hoodlums in Wynwood," Knowlton said when they were alone again. "Oh, Halloween there may be some mischievous damage in the shopping center. But there aren't any bars or special hangouts for young people here in Wynwood. I mean, there are places they go, but they aren't just for kids . . ."

"No beer and jukebox hangouts?" Devery asked.

"Not what I think you mean," Knowlton said. "Oh, there's a quick lunch place in the center with a jukebox that goes all day. It's mostly used by truckers passing through, local workmen during the lunch hour, kids after school for a hamburger and a Coke. They don't sell liquor."

"Holy Grail country," Devery said.

"Oh, they don't have to go too far to find places—in the

next town, over the state line," Knowlton said. "But I—and my kind of people—pay for protection. The troopers here, at our insistence, are really tough on speeders. There are summer dances in the high school gym for young people, but they're supervised. We want it that way, Frank, and that's the way it is."

"And your pistol-packin' mamas keep out-of-towners from getting too noisy," Devery said. "All the same, in the last six weeks you've had a rape attempt, a second attack by a masked idiot firing shots from a gun that was used in a murder six months ago, plus an attack by vandals who tear up a man's clothes and stamp on his toothpaste! Is that the way you want it, Fred?"

Knowlton glanced at Peter. "If the rape and the second attack on the girl ever happened. No, that's not the way I want it."

"I'm getting sick of this 'if it ever happened' department," Peter said. "Explain the vandalism at the camp, Mr. Knowlton, and the threatening note to me. Am I supposed to leave town to prevent me from finding out those things *never* happened? The only possible threat I am to anyone is that I may find out those things *did* happen and who did them!"

Knowlton nodded slowly. "How can I help?"

"You say you're helping three kids in town at the moment," Peter said. "They'll hear all the gossip, all the dirt, what their parents are talking about at the supper table. Try to find out for me what the locals are thinking, Mr. Knowlton. I've got young Ben Gleason from the *Advocate* working for me, but everyone knows he's a reporter and his own friends may clam up on him."

"I'll do what I can," Knowlton said. "Check with me later tonight."

Devery and Peter stood up to go.

"I knew Peter could count on you, Fred," Devery said.

"There's just one problem with me as an undercover

agent," Knowlton said, his smile wry. "The young people I know in this town are likely to tell me what they think I want to hear."

"Or no more trickle down?" Devery asked.

Peter's local contacts on the case seemed to have vanished from the scene that late summer afternoon. A telephone call from the pay phone in the local drugstore to the Wilson house produced what Peter hoped it would, Kay Logan on the other end. Mrs. Wilson's nurse reported that Judith had not come home yet, so she hadn't been able to deliver Peter's message. Brad Smith, the *Advocate's* owner-editor, was back at his desk.

"I was at a town board meeting when you were here, Mr. Styles," he said. "I have no idea where Ben is. I turned him lose to work on your story with you. He wasn't required to check in and he hasn't. But he's got to be in town somewhere. Somebody must have seen him."

Peter realized he wasn't a stranger in Wynwood any longer. He was conscious that people in the drugstore were looking at him as though he were some kind of a movie star. The clerk spoke to him by name.

"Sure, I know Ben, Mr. Styles," he said in answer to a question from Peter. "I haven't seen him all day, but there's no particular reason why I should unless he came in here to buy something."

Peter and Devery drove back down to the camp. Devery's car was there and he had to head back to the city. Tomorrow was press day at *Newsview*. The camp was just as they'd left it, no sign of any visitation in their absence.

"This whole mess is your choice, you know, Peter," Devery said. "It's the town's business. It's the local cop's business. You don't have to sit here and wait for someone to take a crack at you. I'll send you on a story to Timbuctoo if you want an excuse for backing out. I don't want to lose a good man, man."

"You didn't back off on me when senseless violence had me hanging by my fingernails," Peter said. "Judith is counting on me for help."

"You were my close friend," Devery said. "She's a stranger to you."

"That doesn't make her need any less," Peter said.

"I shouldn't have mentioned it," Devery said. "I knew what you'd say. Well, when you've gotta go, you've gotta go. If you need any help I can give you, need me to send someone up here from our shop, let me know."

"Thanks, chum. You know I will; but at the moment I can't think how you can help more than you have."

At the door Devery paused. "There are always coincidences in stories that come our way," he said. "I've learned not to trust them very often. But there's one here that sticks in my craw."

"George Wilson?" Peter asked quietly.

"I should have known you'd be out of the starting gate ahead of me," Devery said. "What was it Dr. Smalley said to you about Judith? She was a target for tragedy? Well, look at it. Her father got killed in an accident. He worked for George Wilson. Her mother fell down the cellar stairs and was turned into a dummy. She was married to George Wilson. Her about-to-be husband was murdered. He was on the verge of becoming George Wilson's son-in-law. The girl was raped. She was George Wilson's stepdaughter. Has it occurred to you, Peter, that George Wilson has been the target for tragedy all along?"

The sound of Devery's departing car had only just died away when the telephone in the camp's living room rang. Peter went in from the deck to answer it. The caller was Fred Knowlton, their host of the afternoon.

"Not thinking about the minor amenities when you were here, Peter," he said. "It occurred to me, after you'd gone, that a picture of the entire community is what you're digging for. I've arranged a guest card for you at the Wynwood Country Club. They have a good restaurant and bar, and people come and go and talk and talk. If you're a guest there you don't have to be introduced to people to—to strike up the band. Gossip in perpetual motion. You'll find your card waiting for you in the front office there."

"Many thanks," Peter said. "It could be helpful. Devery's just gone. My two contacts in town seem to have vanished into the summer sunshine for the moment."

"The girl?" Knowlton asked.

"And young Ben Gleason who works on the *Advocate*. I counted on him as a constant reference source, but he seems to have taken off on some lead of his own."

"Lead to what?" Knowlton asked.

"I wish I knew," Peter said. "My problem at the moment is I don't know who or what I'm looking for, or the faintest notion of where to start."

"You encountered Diane Summers, our local real estate lady?" Knowlton asked.

"Matter of fact I have. The Jordons arranged for her to introduce me to the camp here."

Knowlton chuckled. "Now there's a lady who knows every bit of gossip about everyone in town, rich or poor, rare, medium, and well done. If you can stand hearing twice as much as you want to know, our Diane could be useful."

Any kind of action was better than just sitting here waiting for something to happen, Peter told himself. He called the *Advocate* again. Brad Smith was gone, but a pleasant-sounding woman on the other end told him that Ben Gleason hadn't been in all afternoon. Yes, he had a home phone in his apartment in town. Peter tried that number and got no answer.

Then he called the house on the hill and got what he didn't want, George Wilson. Judith's stepfather wasn't pleased to get the call.

"Miss Logan tells me you've been trying to reach Judith, left messages for her," Wilson said, in an angry voice. "I've tried to tell you as politely as I know how that I don't want you meddling in Judith's problems."

"I'm sorry," Peter said. "She asked me for help. I don't want her to think I've backed off."

"Well, back off!" Wilson almost shouted. "You'll just confuse the poor kid more than she's already confused—you telling her one thing, her doctor and her family telling her something else! I warn you, Mr. Styles, I'll get a court order forcing you to stay away from her. Who the hell do you think you are, barging in where you're not wanted?"

"You haven't already taken some kind of action, have you Wilson?"

"How do you mean?"

"It wasn't you, was it, who invaded the camp here, destroyed my belongings, suggested that I leave town and mind my own business?"

"Oh, for Christ's sake!" Wilson said. "What kind of creep do you think I am?"

"That's something I'm trying to figure out," Peter said.

"Keep interfering with Judith, Styles, and I'll spell it out for you," Wilson said. He jammed down the receiver and the dial tone sounded in Peter's ear.

Not exactly the way to win friends and influence people, Peter thought. The simple truth was that it wasn't too hard to understand George Wilson's resentment. A stranger walks into town and plumps himself down in the center of a difficult and very trying situation, which is in the hands of trained medical men and trained policemen, tilts off-center the mental balance of a girl who has been subjected to unbearable pressures, and insists on continuing to stir up the mud from the bottom of the pond. In Wilson's position Peter knew that he would kick that unwanted stranger out on his ear. Wilson had been hostile from the very start, but, then, he too had been subjected to more pressures than any one man should be asked to endure. There had been a first wife who died of cancer, a second wife hopelessly crippled in an accident, a stepdaughter who resented him and then went off her rocker and became an expensive mental case when her lover was murdered. That was more load than any man could be expected to carry cheerfully. Wilson needed a different kind of handling from Peter than he was getting.

It was about a quarter to five in the afternoon when Peter checked the back door, the windows, and the front-door lock at the camp, and took off for town in his car. Fred Knowlton's suggestion that he talk to the real estate lady might help to get him moving in some profitable direction.

Diane Summers's office was in the front room of a beautiful little cottage on the village green where she also lived. She was just closing up shop for the day when Peter walked in on her.

"Mr. Styles! How nice to see you again," she said.

She was Mrs. Summers, he knew from the Jordons, a widow in her late thirties or early forties. Her hair was a very bright red that had to have come out of a bottle. Her smile was professionally bright. She was wearing a yellow corduroy pantssuit and she had, Peter noticed, the hips and thighs to get away with it. Jewelry seemed to be a part of her image—earrings, a gold chain around her neck with a gold pendant hanging just at the beginning of her cleavage, rings on both hands. Gray-green eyes were speculative, curious. She must have been, some years ago, a pretty dashing piece of stuff, and she was not to be passed by now without an appreciative glance.

"You've been making headlines," she said. "I hope there's nothing wrong at the camp!"

"Things have been happening there," Peter said, "but nothing that requires your professional help. I took a chance that you might let me buy you a drink. Fred Knowlton suggested that you might be able to tell me things about this town that I very much need to know."

"I doubt if Fred Knowlton made me sound like one of his favorite people," she said. She laughed, and there was no resentment in the sound of it. "I'm afraid I've said no to him once too often."

"He didn't hint at anything like that," Peter said. "I have a guest card at the country club and I understand there's a nice bar there. Could I persuade you to show me my way around out there?"

"I'd love to have a drink with you," Diane Summers said, "but not at the country club. You don't know this town, do you, Mr. Styles? Go down the list of members at the country club and you won't find any local names on it. I'm local. I prefer not to go some place where I'm not wanted." There was just a touch of bitterness.

"You name the place," Peter said.

"There's a bar just through that door there in my living room," she said. "Scotch, bourbon, gin, vodka. Will any of those do?"

"That will make it your party."

"Let it be mine this time, Mr. Styles. I'm expecting a phone call about a piece of property I'd like to sell."

The lady liked bright colors. The curtains at her living room windows were a gaudy chintz. There were some rather good Japanese prints on the walls. The rug was a deep purple color, not practical but handsome. The tables and the mantle over the fireplace were cluttered with knickknacks, carved ivory figures, a collection of small stuffed animals, odds and ends of small china saucers and cups. Diane Summers had things here she cared for, without any special design or theme.

"Fred Knowlton used to call this my junk shop," Diane

said. "My husband traveled a lot, business, and he'd bring me things from places where he went. If you've been in Fred's house you know that everything there is carefully planned and designed. I think this room offended him."

"You get the feeling these things are cared for," Peter said. "I like it."

"Bless you. But you didn't come here to look at my gewgaws," the woman said. "What will you drink?"

"Bourbon on the rocks with a dash of plain water—if that's available."

She busied herself at a little bar on wheels in the corner of the room. "The whole town is talking about Judith, and the bullet you found in the tree. We've really had it in Wynwood in the last six months. First the shooting down of Dick Robbins, then someone trying to rape Judith, then last night and this morning. What's got everyone uptight is suddenly knowing that Dick's killer is somewhere around here, after six months."

"Finding the bullet isn't all that's happened today," Peter said. He told her about the vandalism at the camp and the threatening note to him. "One of the things I wanted to ask you, Mrs. Summers, is who might have a key to the camp? There was no sign of a break-in and I left the place locked."

"The only key I know of I turned over to you." She handed him his drink. "My friends call me Di," she said. "Here's how!" She raised her own drink, which was obviously gin or vodka and tonic.

"Would the Jordans have given a key to someone else?" he asked after he'd tasted his drink.

"I think they'd have told me if they had," Di Summers said. "I was showing the place, you know, for rental. I had just found a customer for it when they cabled me from London that you were to have it."

"So I cheated you out of a commission?"

"Bob Jordan isn't that kind of a guy. He sent me a check."

Di sat down opposite her guest. "What did Fred Knowlton think I could do for you, Peter?"

"I don't smell very good to George Wilson, to the police, or to the two medical men I've met."

"Smalley and Kreuger?"

He nodded. "They've had the last six months you talked about all wrapped up in a neat Christmas package. Dick Robbins was shot to death by some crook cruising through town. There never was any rape attack on Judith. It was something she dreamed up in a sick mind. They didn't believe she was attacked again last night, and both the troopers and the doctors were at some pains to make that clear to me. Then, this morning, Judith and I found the bullet, which backed up her story. They still choose not to believe it, or if last night happened it was just someone playing games with a disturbed girl. Wilson has ordered me to stay away from Judith. Dr. Kreuger says he would be an expert witness in court to testify that the rape never happened. But someone wants me to stop looking any further for what I think is the truth. That truth for me is that everything Judith has said in the past and about last night is the truth, that there is a killer in Wynwood, and that he's taken aim at me. But where do I start looking? I think Fred Knowlton thought that's where you might be helpful."

Di Summers sipped her drink and looked pleased with it. "There used to be an old British colonel who lived here," she said. "Full of stories about World War Two, and particularly about Winston Churchill, whom he could imitate marvelously. It seems someone was making an interminable speech in the House of Commons one day. Churchill turned to his secretary and asked who the speaker was. 'New member, sir,' the secretary said, 'making his maiden speech. Alfred Bossom. B-O-S-S-O-M.' Churchill, according to our colonel, muttered: 'Bossom?

Bossom! Why, that's neither the one thing nor the other!' " Di laughed at her own joke. "That's me, Peter; neither the one thing nor the other. I'm not fancy enough to join their elite country club; but if they have a problem, good old Di is the one to turn to for help."

"You're not obligated to help me, Di," Peter said.

"Glad to if I can," she said. "But not because Fred Knowlton asks it. I'm not good enough to move in his social world, but I don't know what I'm missing if I won't let him into my bed!"

"I don't wonder at the impulse," Peter said.

"Now, now, Peter, I don't know you well enough yet for that to be on our agenda. You want to know if I think you're way off base about Judith Larsen?"

"Do you?"

"Let me tell you what I think and have thought for the last six weeks," Di said. "I think she was attacked and roughed up by some giant goon in a ski mask six weeks ago. I think she was approached by a second man in a ski mask last night and was lucky enough to get to you for help. And I think I know why you are being pressured to drop the case and leave town."

"I love you," Peter said.

"Don't be casual with words like that," she said, smiling at him. "I might take you seriously and change the subject, from Judith to us."

"There is a time for everything," Peter said.

She took another sip of her drink. "So, let's finish with Judith, which involves a primary lesson about the beautiful town of Wynwood. I am local, but I know many of the rich residents because I handle most of their property transactions. That makes me the local Alfred Bossom, neither the one thing nor the other. In the process I have come to know this town, which, I suggest to you, is like most other places, only more so! It is set up for the privileged, by the privileged. The rest of us serve them. The difference here and some other places is that Wynwood is such a small town that the division between the rich and the locals is constantly visible, right in front of our noses."

"Which is getting us where, Di?"

"Let me put it to you this way. The locals, from childhood on up, are pretty damn well behaved. Not because they are special, but because you get the hell kicked out of you if you misbehave. The town cops are set up to protect the rich, their property, and their peace and quiet. Ditto the troopers. If a local young person raises hell, he's promptly punished, and the chances are his family, depending on the rich for work, will find themselves out of a job. Retaliation against the locals for anything just a little off base is swift and hard. But if someone in the rich families raises some kind of hell it's hushed up, handled with kid gloves, covered up. Let a local be arrested for driving drunk and he'll lose his license. Let a rich guy get arrested for the same thing and the cop will drive him home!"

"Which relates to Judith how?" Peter asked.

"She's local," Di said. "I've got to make something clear to you, Peter. I'm not saying the locals are all saints, forced to be by the people they serve. I'm just saying they don't misbehave or raise hell *in* Wynwood. Everybody has wheels today. You don't have to go very far to find places where you can hoot 'n holler without offending the Knowltons, or the Steeles, or the Koblers, and the rest of them. Which, my patient friend, brings me back to Judith. What happened to her happened only a half a mile from the very center of town. She was attacked, stripped of her clothes, mauled, fondled, tossed around—just half a mile from the village green. Tell you anything, Peter?"

"That the attacker wasn't local? Forbidden territory?"

"For that you get an A," Di said. She was smiling but her

smile, Peter thought, had taken on a kind of frozen quality. "My husband died about seven years ago, Peter. Diabetes. We had no kids. Mike was afraid of passing his problem on. I was thirty-two, very much alive, still reasonably attractive, right out in the store window because I had to make a living for myself."

"Seven years haven't made you less attractive," Peter said.

"Thank you, sir. If you're not careful I will get off the subject, which is Judith, not me. But my experience, over the last seven years, has given me a notion of what Judith may have faced in the last six months. She's an attractive girl; her man is dead. That makes her free game for anyone on the rich side of the tracks who wants to have at her. It's happened to me, ad nauseum. I've been propositioned by old and young. I've had this cottage broken into in the middle of the night by young studs—and old studs—who think I was invented to give them pleasure. If I named you names, you wouldn't believe me. And let me tell you, Peter, if I brought charges against any of them for invading my privacy I'd be out of business, driven out of town. They band together like a club! They have the best lawyers money can buy. Not only that, my own people, local people, would be on their side. The rich would bring pressure on them to bring pressure on me. You begin to get a picture?"

Peter wasn't smiling. "It begins to take shape," he said. "You're suggesting Judith was attacked by someone on the rich side of the tracks. The cops, the troopers, the Smalleys and Kreugers suspect that. Since she can't name anybody, they write it off by declaring that she's a hysterical neurotic."

Di nodded. "And George Wilson, her stepfather, goes along with them. His very existence depends on the services he provides for the rich club. Let him stir up the smooth surface of the water and he'd be out of business overnight. The girl wasn't critically hurt, wasn't really raped in their terms. If Wilson tried to force the police to dig deeper, he'd be gone. So he plays along. What else can he do? Then, last night—"

"They plan to write that off, too, since she wasn't hurt," Peter said.

Di nodded. "But you made a problem for them," she said. "Famous investigative reporter who won't let go of a story until he's run it to earth. Five minutes after you go to the troopers, they have you off on the road to buying their story. Dr. Smalley is a decent old man I think, but they've sold him. Kreuger's something else again. A brilliant doctor, but I'll bet he has his price. The rich support his clinic, pay him his enormous fees. If you hadn't found the bullet in the tree this morning, Peter, they might finally have convinced you. Now the apple cart is really overturned. You won't give up, and reporters from all over the country will be here by tomorrow. The rich man's club is going to be invaded by people who insist on answers. And the troopers, knowing now that Dick Robbins's killer is still in the neighborhood, aren't going to sit back and do nothing."

"Destroying my belongings and telling me to leave town isn't a smart way to get rid of me," Peter said.

"We've been talking in Wynwood about a disturbed and crazy girl for the last six weeks," Di said. "What we really have, I think, is a disturbed and crazy member of the rich man's club."

"Or two members," Peter said. "Judith is certain last night's man isn't the same one who attacked her six weeks ago."

"The average citizen today reads about young people who mug and rob and rape and set fires, and they just assume its not their kind of kids," Di said. "They assume they're blacks, or Hispanics, or drug addicts, or sex perverts from another world. Not their kids, and surely not the young people in the rich men's club who wear Brooks Brothers' clothes and custom-made shoes."

"But you think they exist right here in Wynwood?"

"Oh so carefully shielded from the public eye," Di said. "But I can tell you from personal experience that you don't have to go a mile down the road to find alcoholics, drug addicts, and sex perverts. Some of them have gone too far with Judith, and thanks to you, some very important people in the world of money are really sweating it out this evening. You should be warned, Peter, that they have the means and the know-how to fight back, legally or illegally. Whatever it takes."

"So I should pack up and leave town?"

She eyes him steadily. "But you won't."

"No, Di, I won't."

"So we should have another drink on that," she said, took his glass and hers, and crossed over to the bar. "I may have given you the wrong impression about Fred Knowlton. He's not a villain, Peter. He and I just didn't—didn't hit it off. I didn't want to play it his way." She came back with their drinks. "He has no children to protect."

"That's not quite as I understood it," Peter said. "Dick Robbins was like a son to him, and I understand he's helping other youngsters here in Wynwood."

"Locals," she said. "Haven't I convinced you you're not up against locals? I think you can count on Fred to help you if the trail leads to capturing Dick Robbins's killer. He's the only one in the rich men's club who might turn against his friends, his peers, if one of them was in any way connected with Dick Robbins's death."

"And you?" Peter asked. "Can I come back to you to learn what you may hear as we go along?"

She smiled. "I could hope you might come back for some other reason," she said, "but I suppose I must be satisfied with whatever brings you."

He didn't go just then. Later he wished he had. They talked, she about herself, he about himself and the grim reasons that had made him a crusader against violence in all its forms. In the end she made him supper and it was long after dark when he took off once more for the camp. Before he left her he called Ben Gleason's home phone without luck. It worried him a little that he had been out of touch with Judith and young Gleason for so long. There might be some kind of message from one of them at the camp. He knew that if he stayed on with Di Summers he might find himself in a delightful involvement with her. This was not the time for it.

Unlike the night before, clouds covered the moon and the woods leading down to the camp were pitch dark. He had left in daylight so there were no lights in the house. A kind of uneasiness he hadn't felt for a long time seemed to take over when he parked the Toyota by the house and switched off the headlights. Someone could be watching, waiting.

He closed the car door quietly and stood beside it for a moment, listening. A hoot owl made noises in the darkness around him. He selected his door key on his key ring, went up the steps to the deck, and walked around to the front door. He unlocked the door and stepped into the house. He found the light switch to the right on the door and switched it on.

He froze.

A man was lying on the living room floor in front of the fireplace. He wasn't recognizable because over his head was a brown, cloth ski mask.

The man didn't move. The opening and closing of the door hadn't disturbed him. Peter walked very slowly over to the man and stood beside him.

"Hey, you!" Peter said.

There was no response. Peter knelt down beside him and picked up a hand. He felt for a pulse but couldn't detect one. He reached out, took hold of the cloth hood, and pulled it off.

"Oh, Jesus!" Peter whispered.

Ben Gleason stared up at him with wide-open dead eyes. In the center of the young man's forehead was what Peter knew was a bullet hole.

PART THREE

1

There come moments when people who are conditioned to violence, like cops, like soldiers in a war zone, are not able to take what they come on in a cold, impersonal, professional way. The victim can be a cop's partner, and that surviving partner can't quite handle it. The victim can be the soldier who went though basic training with a friend, shared breakfast with him just that morning, faced enemy bullets with him the day before. It's not the same as a body in a ditch beside the road, passed by almost unnoticed by advancing troops. The personal involvement makes the shock so much harder to weather.

Peter had known Ben Gleason for less than twenty-four hours, but they were involved together, working on the same problem, same story. Peter wondered whether, if Ben hadn't thrown in his lot with a stranger, he would be lying there on the hearth, staring blindly up at the ceiling.

An impersonal voice at the trooper barracks took Peter's first report. Then a dazed-sounding Brad Smith, editor of the *Advocate* got the news and promised he was on the way.

"Does the boy have a family?" Peter asked.

"Not here in Wynwood," Smith said. "There may be an address among his personal belongings or in his desk at the paper. I'll see what I can find. Christ, what a thing, Mr. Styles!"

Peter waited. There was nothing else to do that might not interfere with a proper police investigation. For the second time in a day someone had gained entry to the locked camp without any indication of a break-in. There was no sign of any sort of violence in the room. Either Ben Gleason had been lured here—a false message from Peter?—and shot when he arrived by a killer who was waiting for him, or he had been killed somewhere else and brought here and left like a sort of calling card. Why else the ski mask?

And then they came, trooper cars with sirens wailing, others following in their wake. There was the slamming of car doors, the clatter of feet on the deck outside, and then Sergeant Mike Quinlan came in, followed by a small army of troopers and nonuniformed men. Old Dr. Jonathan Smalley was one of them.

Everybody stood silent for a moment, staring down at the body. Then Dr. Smalley approached and knelt beside what was left of Ben Gleason.

"Stadler's on his way," Quinlan said to Peter. "I'm 'it' for the time being. You said on the phone you found him here?"

"Unlocked the front door, switched on the lights, and there he was."

"Just as he is now?"

"No. He was wearing that ski mask there on the rug beside him. I thought it was a stranger, drunk, drugged out. I shouted at him and when there wasn't any response I felt for a pulse. There was none. I pulled off the ski mask. After that I've touched nothing but the telephone."

Dr. Smalley stood up, wiping his hands on a handkerchief. "He's dead," the old man said, his voice angry. Ben Gleason had been his friend. "For some time, I'd guess. Unofficially, until we perform an autopsy, the cause of death is a gunshot wound in the head. It would have been like a bomb going off in his skull." He turned to Peter. "I'm the medical examiner in Wynwood, called in whenever there is an untimely death."

"Untimely!" Peter said.

"Official language for a murder," Dr. Smalley said. He turned back to Quinlan. "When you're finished with him you can take him over to the morgue, Sergeant."

Finished with him!

Photographs, fingerprints, and questions. One photograph with the ski mask pulled back over Ben Gleason's head, just as Peter had found him. Quinlan took Peter over to a far corner of the room. He was as impersonal as if they'd never had a drink together, never had any kind of contact before.

"When did you leave here before you came back and found him?" was the first question.

It had been a little before five in the afternoon. Peter had driven up to town, tried to locate Gleason and Judith Larsen without any luck. He'd then gone to talk to Diane Summers and actually spent several hours with her.

"Trying to get a picture of the town from her," Peter said. "Fred Knowlton suggested her as a source."

He made it clear that before he'd left the camp he'd made sure everything was locked. After the earlier invasion by vandals it hadn't been a casual check. So far he hadn't left this room to check once more on the back door, the garage entrance. But the front door had been locked, just as he'd left it, when he came back.

"The ski mask?" Quinlan asked. "You ever see it before?"

"No."

"I mean, could it have belonged to the Jordans, been here in the camp?"

"I have no way of knowing."

"Gleason would fit the description of the man Judith Larsen said approached her last night," Quinlan said. "Slim, agile, energetic."

"Oh, for God's sake," Peter said. "You know Gleason!"

One of the troopers came over from where the men were working with their cameras and dusting powders. He was carrying the ski mask.

"He wasn't wearing this when he was shot," the trooper told Quinlan. "No bullet hole. Must have been pulled on over his head after he was dead. Blood stains on the inside, but no hole."

"Which suggests Ben wasn't creeping around wearing that mask," Peter said. "He was shot here or brought here after he was shot, the mask added afterward."

"Thanks for pointing out the obvious," Quinlan said.

"He came here this past morning, as you know, and discovered the vandalism. He brought me here to see it. Dr. Smalley will confirm that. Later we went up to town, visited with Brad Smith, and then went to call on Dr. Kreuger. After that we split—no particular plan. He was just going to listen around in town. He never did get in touch again. Nor have I been able, by the way, to locate Judith Larsen. That concerns me, in the face of this."

"Why?"

Peter was suddenly angry with this stone-faced young officer. "If you would just pull the plug and let your tired theories go down the drain!" he said. "What has to happen for you to accept the fact that you've all been wrong about Judith? She's told you the truth from the start and for one reason or another you all choose not to believe her. I believe her and I have been threatened. The vandalism was a threat and this is a threat, or why leave Ben here for me to find? Ben had decided to believe her and he's dead! Do you have to have a cement block dropped on your head, Quinlan?"

Quinlan took it without the slightest change in expression. "I'm listening," he said.

"Judith left the Wilson place in her car shortly after you and Stadler finished questioning her—early afternoon. She hadn't come back by four-thirty in the afternoon. I'd left a message with Fay Logan for her to get in touch with me. It was never delivered because Judith hadn't come back. Later I talked to George Wilson. He threatened me with a court action if I didn't leave Judith alone. I don't know now whether she's back and safe, or whether she's still missing."

"She wouldn't leave her mother for too long," Quinlan said.

"I hope."

"I'll find out," Quinlan said. "I want her to look at that ski mask to see if its the same kind she claimed she saw last night—and six weeks ago."

He left Peter and went over to the phone on the desk in the corner of the room. The place was crowded with men at work and Peter couldn't hear, over the noise of their back-and-forth talk, what Quinlan was saying to someone on the phone. Eventually, the sergeant rejoined Peter.

"I got George Wilson," he said. He was frowning. "Judith didn't come home for supper, isn't there now. Wilson doesn't know where she is, but he doesn't seem worried about it, even after I told him what had happened here. He says they've been trying to persuade Judith to go away somewhere for a while, get out of the atmosphere here. I know from my wife that Dr. Kreuger has been trying to convince her to do just that."

"So she just takes off without telling anyone she's going, or where she's going?"

"She doesn't have any contact with Wilson. It's a pity, considering how generous he's been to her mother—and to her. Kay Logan says she always tells her mother where she's going even though it doesn't register. This afternoon, according to Wilson, Miss Logan was in the kitchen getting something for her patient when Judith took off. She didn't hear, as she often does, Judith telling her mother where she was going and when she'd be back."

"So you're not worried?" Peter asked.

Quinlan looked down at his right hand, which was folded into a clenched fist. "Let's you and me start over, Styles," he said. "You began giving Nora and me trouble last night, and you complicated that this morning when you found that bullet. We both wonder if you may not be right. That's why she got you in to see Dr. Kreuger. Maybe we've been off base all along."

"Thank God somebody is beginning to wonder about that," Peter said. "I think she knew I was her friend, ready to go to bat for her. Why would she just take off without telling me?"

"Truth or not, she's a mixed-up girl," Quinlan said.

"She wouldn't leave her mother before. Why now?"

"Afraid of something," Quinlan suggested.

"Then why not ask for help? She had me to ask. I think she trusted me."

"That girl has been in a hysterical state for months, ever since Dick Robbins was killed," Quinlan said. "I don't blame her, you understand, but you can't count on her to do the expected."

"I'd like to find her, just to be sure," Peter said. "If she's all right and wants to stay out of sight that's her business. But this isn't some kid's game that's being played around here, Quinlan. Until I know that wherever she is she's there voluntarily, I'm not going to rest easy."

"We'll put out an alarm for her if Wilson insists he doesn't know where she is," Quinlan said. "He may just be trying to help her stay out of trouble." He gave Peter a narrowed-eyed smile. "You feel safe yourself, Peter? Somebody is sure as hell trying to send you a message."

Peter glanced across the room where troopers and two ambulance attendants were lifting Ben Gleason's body onto a stretcher. "That's what happens to anyone who gets on the trail of what's going on in this hellhole. No, I don't feel safe, but I'm not going anywhere."

The bearers were almost at the door with the stretcher when it opened and Brad Smith, Ben Gleason's boss, came in out of what was now a rainy night. He asked a question, lifted the blanket that covered the body, and turned away like a man who was about to be sick. Dr. Smalley put his hand on the editor's shoulder.

"I'm sorry, Brad," the old man said. "But know it was quick. No pain."

"If the poor kid wasn't scared out of his wits before it happened," Smith said. He saw Peter and Quinlan across the room and came over to them. "His parents are living out in Scottsdale, Arizona. I found their address in the office. I had the unpleasant job of calling them on the phone and telling them. Why, Mike? Why did it happen to him?"

"Styles thinks he got onto something," Quinlan said.

"Did he hint at something, Mr. Styles?" Smith asked.

Peter shook his head. "When we left you about lunchtime we went to the clinic to see Kreuger. After that we split. He had nothing on his mind then, and I was never in touch with him again. There must be a way to backtrack on his afternoon, where he went, who he talked with. Everybody in town knows him."

"We can spread the word, ask the question," Smith said. "There are people I imagine are friends of yours, Mr. Styles, moving in on us—reporters from the big-city papers and radio and TV. This will make for a field day when it catches up with them. Incidentally, Mike, Ben wasn't a skier. His winter sports were squash and paddle tennis. I'd bet my life he didn't own a ski mask."

"Unless he bought it to play games with Judith Larsen," Quinlan said.

"Oh, come on, Mike! You don't believe that for a minute, do you?"

"No, I don't," Quinlan said. "But in my business you bring up everything just in order to write it off. Isn't that how it is with you, Styles?"

"If it helps get you to a starting point," Peter said.

At that moment Captain Stadler arrived and Quinlan left Peter and Brad Smith to join his superior. There were dark circles under Smith's eyes as though he'd been on an all-night binge.

"Such a hell of a nice kid," he said, almost as if he was talking to himself. "Reporters don't get killed for doing a routine job."

"Routine?" Peter asked.

Smith glanced up. "I see what you mean. The bullet, which tells us that Dick Robbins's murderer may still be in town. A lead to who owns the gun would not be 'routine,' would it?"

"He hadn't the faintest notion about such a lead when I last saw him," Peter said. "How do we start checking on his afternoon?"

Smith glanced at his wristwatch. "It's going on eleven. This is an early-to-bed town normally, but with this story breaking—"

"But two o'clock this afternoon," Peter said. "The vandalism had taken place here in broad daylight. That was the thing we were after when we separated at the clinic. Who saw or heard what gossip? Where would Ben have gone for that kind of information?"

"The local bars," Smith said, "the drugstore, the shopping center." He smiled faintly. "I taught him early that there were a couple of infallible sources for gossip in Wynwood—a couple of old ladies who sit in rocking chairs on their front porches in summertime, see everything, hear damn near everything. Ben had cultivated them well; used to be served cookies and milk while they gave him all the dirt they'd been able to scrounge. But they couldn't have seen anything related to the vandalism. None of those front porches overlook the camp here."

"Nobody overlooks the camp," Peter said. Then his eyes widened. "There's a young man who seems to live out on the lake just beyond my door—little boat with a red sail. Waves at me when I come and go. I think Ben said his name was Steele."

"Billy Steele, Cyrus Steele's son," Smith said.

"Could Ben have gone to him to ask if he saw anyone hanging around this place?"

"He might," Smith said. "I think they were friends, played squash together in winter."

"Locals and the rich mixing?"

"Young people aren't so socially minded," Smith said. "Everyone liked Ben, God help us."

"So he didn't have enemies, he just discovered something!"

"Which he found out after you left the clinic at two o'clock in the afternoon," Smith said. "Let me cover the old ladies, if they're still up and around. If Billy Steele isn't at home you'll probably find him at the country club. Bar stays open there till two o'clock. But there'll be talk everywhere, Mr. Styles. Every place that's open in the area will be buzzing." Smith shook his head. "Everyone will have seen Ben somewhere, but heard nothing real. Everyone will want to get into the act, be important. Poor Ben, he was so thrilled at the chance to work with you, Mr. Styles."

"And I just may have gotten him killed," Peter said, his voice harsh. "I persuaded him to help me keep something alive that someone wants kept dead."

"You shouldn't blame yourself, Mr. Styles. He was doing a reporter's job."

Doing a reporter's job wasn't possible for Peter at the moment. Captain Stadler wasn't interested in him except as someone implicated in a murder case. He was irritated by Peter's insistence that locating Judith Larsen was a primary project.

"We've been operating some kind of a care center for that crazy broad for weeks now," the captain said. "You insist you have no idea, Styles, where Gleason was headed, who he planned to interview, what he thought, or suspected, or guessed at about the vandalism here earlier? Because that's what you two were concerned with, wasn't it, the vandalism?"

"Which came about because I chose to believe Judith Larsen, and opened up the Robbins case again. There's no other reason why anyone in Wynwood should have the remotest interest in me. So Judith is important, and where she is right now concerns me."

"Vandalism doesn't always have a sensible motive," Stadler said. "Kids just break into some place, foul it up."

"You forget there was a message to me—get out of town and mind my own business. Now that message is even clearer, wouldn't you say, Captain? Someone who was helping me meddle in that business I was warned to avoid is shot dead, brought here and left on my hearthstone, with a kind of signpost that tells us exactly why he's dead."

"Signpost?"

"The ski mask, man! Do you need it written out in words of one syllable? Ben Gleason had got on the trail of something connected to the Judith Larsen case. The ski mask tells us that. You know that someone fired at Judith last night with a gun that was used to murder one of your men. It's a hundred-to-one that when you solve this killing you'll have solved the other. But damn it, Stadler, Judith's at the very center of the whole mess and nobody, including her stepfather, thinks it's worth bothering to look for her!"

"It isn't midnight yet," Stadler said. "That's not late for young people to be out and around. She took off in her car, I understand. She could be visiting friends in the next town. She can have gone to a late movie in Torrington or Great Barrington or over in Bantam. She wouldn't hear what's happened if that's where she is. She'll turn up."

"This isn't any night!" Peter said, fighting his impatience. "This is the night when a man who was checking out her story is murdered in cold blood and left here to tell me to back off."

"We'll put out an alarm for her," Stadler finally agreed. "If she's had a car accident, it should have been reported in to the barracks."

"There are a lot of things that should happen that don't

happen," Peter said. "George Wilson should be demanding that you find her, not me."

Stadler looked, suddenly, like a very tired man. "I imagine it's hard for an outsider to understand George," he said. "I've known him for fifteen years, ever since I first came to work in this district. He was once a bright, hard-working, always cheerful guy. He set up a business here that started with mowing lawns for a buck an hour when he was a kid and built it into a service that the whole community depends on. He's hired to take care of and protect the homes of people who don't trust just anyone. I guess you could say he's Wynwood's leading local citizen, respected by the rich people who have, you could say, bought out his town. Then the world began to cave in on George. His first wife with whom he was very much in love, died. It changed him. There weren't any more jokes or bright sayings. His business grew, but he was alone. No more fun and games. Then Rose Larsen, the widow of one of his good workmen, came into his life. Everyone who knew them was delighted. They both needed someone and it seemed a perfect solution."

"Except to Judith," Peter said.

Stadler looked back over the room where his men were still photographing and dusting. It seemed to Peter that this hard-faced trooper was showing a human side he hadn't expected.

"I thought the child should have her behind spanked," Stadler said. "George talked to me about it once. The protective service he runs for some of the big estates crosses my path, professionally, from time to time. A small robbery, a knocked-down fence post, indirect complaints about some sort of trespassing. This particular day he came to my office about something and he got to talking about his personal problem. Judith was driving him off his rocker. She wouldn't accept him, wouldn't talk to him, tried to escape eating meals with the family. He'd done everything he knew to make her content and happy, but she resented him and resented her mother's having taken on a man to replace her dead father. He talked of the time when she'd be old enough to send away to college. Some contact with the real world might change her. I felt sorry for him. What should have turned out fine for everyone involved almost daily misery for all of them thanks to a neurotic, unreasonable child." Stadler drew a deep breath. "Then the roof really caved in. Rose had her accident."

"How did that happen?" Peter asked.

"We were involved, of course," Stadler said. "At first we thought it could be an attempt at what we call an 'untimely death.' But it was accident, pure and simple. It was after supper—after dark. Judith, as she often did, had supper in her room. She was doing homework. George was involved with some paper work, which he chose to do at the dining room table. Rose was in the kitchen just beyond him. They were talking back and forth from time to time, George told us. She was planning to bake some kind of a pie for the next day. She had some ingredients she'd made in advance and frozen. They were in the freezer down in the basement. She told George she was going down to get what she needed. He offered to go for her, but she told him to stick to his work. A moment later he heard her scream, heard the ugly thudding sound as she fell. That was that. It would have been better if the fall had killed her. You've seen her?"

Peter nodded.

"Judith was no help to him," Stadler said. "It was as if she thought he was somehow at fault."

"How?"

"He should have gone down for her. God knows what she thought. I don't think she's ever spoken to George since then unless it was absolutely necessary. But she stayed a part of the household because her mother survived, in a manner of speaking. Then she had her own disaster, Dick Robbins. George did everything he could for her. They tried to persuade her to go away somewhere—Kreuger, Dr. Smalley. What I'm trying to tell you, Styles, is that the fact that Judith hasn't been home since early afternoon isn't significant. It's part of her pattern not to tell George where she's going or when she'll be back. He's not as concerned as you think he should be because things are no different than they have been for a long time."

"I don't quite buy that, Captain," Peter said. "In the last twenty-four hours she's been attacked again by someone in a ski mask. A shot has been fired at her by the gun that killed her fiancé. And she had a friend she could turn to for help, me."

"I think you'll hear from her," Stadler said. "Wherever she is, the news about Gleason will get to her. It's spreading around town like a forest fire. When she leaves her friends, or the movie theater where she is, someone will tell her about Ben Gleason, or she'll hear it on her car radio. She'll be in touch."

"I hope you're right," Peter said.

"Now I have some advice for you," Stadler said. He was the cold police officer again. "Stay out of this, Styles. Let us handle it. I urge you to go back to the city, go back to New York. Someone thinks you're close to some kind of facts. Are you?"

"Not a notion of any facts," Peter said.

"So drop it. This lunatic, whoever he is, thinks you're on to something. You stay here, keep prying, I can't guarantee he won't come after you. I could place you in protective custody if you refuse. I can't supply you with a constant bodyguard. Not enough manpower. We'll have this place and the woods surrounding it watched tonight, but we can't keep it covered forever."

"I've never run out on a story in my whole career," Peter said.

"You own a gun?" Stadler said.

"No."

"Come back to the barracks with me and I'll issue a license for a weapon," Stadler said. "Everyone else in this town has a license to carry a gun. That might give you a chance if you insist on being stubborn."

It is axiomatic that the professional criminal tries to avoid a situation where he has to attack a policeman. Cops don't like cop killers and when one of their own is wasted the case is never closed until the killer is arrested, convicted, and sentenced. It's perhaps less often referred to, but there is the same kind of tradition by which reporters in the world press, radio, and television live. Let a reporter be killed on the job and his brothers in the profession aren't likely ever to give up until someone has paid for the crime. Perhaps the death of a young boy, working on a small-town weekly newspaper wouldn't attract enough attention to mobilize big-time reporters, but Ben Gleason's connection with Peter Styles made it something else again.

"Comforting if you're dealing with a professional hit man, but meaningless if you're dealing with a nut," Frank Devery said over the phone to Peter.

The trooper and the medical people were gone from the camp. Peter had called Devery in New York. The story of Ben Gleason's murder was already on the news ticker in Devery's office.

"If you want to sit there at an open window with a light shining behind you you'll make a perfect target," Devery said. "Take Stadler's advice and let them handle it."

"I've made two friends in this miserable town," Peter said. "One is dead and one is, I hope, just missing! They counted on me, Frank."

"You won't be any good to the girl dead, with a ski mask

pulled over your head," Devery said. "Any ballistic report on the bullet yet? It was the same gun?"

"Too soon, or, at least, I don't know," Peter said. "Speaking of guns, Stadler offered to issue me a permit."

"What can you lose?" Devery said. "It might just give you an edge. You're determined to stay on it?"

"Yes."

"Just remember, as you go down for the third time, that I've always thought you were a gallant idiot," Devery said. "Stay in touch, Peter—like all the time, chum."

And so he was alone in the camp. A gentle summer rain came down in a steady patter on the unroofed deck outside the windows. Looking out, Peter saw lights crisscrossing the woods. A trooper car just out back of the camp had its headlights focused up the hill from the camp. Another, parked up near the highway, had its lights slanting down across the area. Devery's "nut" wasn't likely to be circulating out there.

Doing nothing was intolerable. Peter found a raincoat and hat belonging to Bob Jordan in the hall closet, put them on, and went out onto the deck. He locked the front door behind him, testing it carefully. As he turned the corner of the house a bright searchlight was turned full on his face. It was operated from the trooper car down below.

"Mr. Styles?"

"Yes."

"Let us know when you're on the move! We're all a little jumpy."

Peter walked down the steps to where the car was parked. His Toyota was just beyond it. The trooper, standing beside his car kept the hand-controlled search focused steadily on Peter.

"Trooper Moffet, Mr. Styles," he said.

Peter explained that he was on the way to the barracks to take Stadler up on his offer of a gun permit.

"I'll follow you," Moffet said, getting back into his car.

"I don't imagine there'll be any trouble between here and the barracks."

"Just the same, I'll stay with you till Stadler passes you on to somebody else," Moffet said.

Peter drove up the hill to the top of the driveway, Moffet behind him. The second trooper car was parked by the entrance, lights shining down across the woods. Evidently, Moffet had contacted the second trooper on his car radio, because the man just waved as Peter drove out onto the main road.

The village of Wynwood was very different from what it had been last night about this same time. Peter didn't see a totally darkened house anywhere. The town was up and buzzing. Behind every lighted window people were discussing a new murder committed by someone who'd obviously been living in their midst for months. Maybe there had been a rape six weeks ago! Maybe there had been a second attempt last night! Maybe there was a psycho prowling around just outside their locked and bolted doors! Wynwood was awake, alert, anxious. At least two trooper cars patrolled the village green, back and forth.

Stadler was in his office, standing by a map of the town and another of the county on a far wall. He was issuing orders to half a dozen troopers about the routes they were to cover on a special patrol set up for the rest of the night.

"Moffet told me on his car radio you were coming in for that gun permit we mentioned," Stadler said. He picked it up from his desk and held it out to Peter. "That'll get you a gun at the local hardware store in the morning."

"Thanks," Peter said.

"You're making a headache for us and I'm not sure I have to put up with it," Stadler said. "I haven't got the manpower or the wheels to keep you covered round the clock. Our switchboard is lit up like a Christmas tree, half the people in town calling in to ask for protection."

"Protection from what?"

"A psycho killer, of course. If they'll stay at home, indoors, away from lighted windows, we can do a pretty good job. If they go out on the town, all start playing cops and robbers, we can't promise to be too effective. I can't promise you anything, Styles, unless you stay put in one place. I can offer you a nice clean bed here in a cell in the barracks. Take an army to get at you here."

"Where is Judith Larsen?"

"Hasn't come home yet. I talked to George Wilson just before you showed up. He thinks she may have taken off for good for a while."

"Where did Ben Gleason spend his afternoon and evening?"

"We're asking around," Stadler said.

"And?"

"So far, nothing," Stadler said.

"Doesn't it seem strange to you that nobody appears to have seen a popular, known-to-everyone young man who was looking for something here in town, had no reason at all to leave town without letting Brad Smith know, or me know, hasn't been seen by anyone since early afternoon? At the same time a girl, whose case Ben was investigating, also hasn't been seen since early afternoon. That doesn't bother you?"

"Naturally I'm bothered that we haven't been able to pick up Ben Gleason's trail," Stadler said. "It's been slow going. People who work in the local bars and eating joints in the early afternoon aren't on the night shift. People on the job now weren't working when Gleason seems to have disappeared in the early afternoon. Our troopers on regular road patrol in the afternoon have been questioned. Most of them know Gleason well; he's in and out of here questioning them about car accidents, disturbances in bars, domestic squabbles—anything on the police blotter. It just happens nobody remembers seeing him around anywhere, in town, or driving the roads. It'll turn up, but it's slow."

"And Judith?"

"Damn it, Styles, we haven't any reason to believe she hasn't gone somewhere of her own free will. If she has she wouldn't report to her stepfather. They, for Christ's sake, don't talk to each other! It's not a family routine for her to check with him. You say you're her friend. Well, if she *isn't* in trouble she'd have no reason to get in touch with you."

"And if she is in trouble maybe she can't," Peter said.

"Let's wait a little while before we start compounding our troubles," Stadler said. "Wilson has promised to let me know the minute she turns up at the house."

"You do concede there's a connection between Gleason's murder and Judith's experiences of the past few weeks?"

Stadler made an impatient gesture. "I concede someone wants us to think that," he said. "The ski mask. I think it's more likely a psycho crazy is trying to confuse us, and Judith, by wandering off somewhere, has played into his hands. You don't buy that?"

"Every instinct I have," Peter said, after a pause, "tells me no. But I suppose it could be."

The office door opened and Dr. Smalley came in, followed by Sergeant Quinlan. The old doctor seemed a little disconcerted to see Peter there. He had a sheaf of papers in his hands, which he put down in front of Stadler on the desk.

"Not quite what we expected," the old doctor said.

Stadler glanced at the papers, scowling. "I don't know what 'off the record' means to you, Styles," he said.

"It means I don't print or pass along what you may tell me to anyone else."

"Good. So this is 'off the record.' Not that it's so earth-shaking." Stadler slapped at the papers with the back of his hand. "You want to play along, or must I tell you to step outside?"

"I'll play along," Peter said.

"It wasn't the same gun," Stadler said.

The doctor and Quinlan were released to speak.

"Different caliber," Quinlan said. "The gun that killed Dick Robbins and that was fired into that tree last night was a .22. The bullet that killed Gleason came from a .38."

"Different killer," Dr. Smalley said.

"All this tells us, Doc, is that it was a different gun," Quinlan said. "People collect guns around here. The killer could own a hatful."

"I can't be too precise about the time of death," the doctor said. "Rigor was pretty well advanced. I got him on the table about a quarter to eleven. I'd guess he's been dead six to eight hours. That would make the time of death sometime between three and five. I'd say it was more likely to have been earlier than later."

"I dropped Ben off at the *Advocate* office so he could get his car after we left the clinic," Peter said. "A little after two. Are you saying he could have been killed within an hour of that time, Doctor?" Peter asked.

The doctor nodded. "More likely then than later," he said.

"I went straight from the newspaper office to the Jordan's camp," Peter said. "I'd left a key for my boss, Frank Devery, at the *Advocate* and he had picked it up and was waiting for me. So for sure Ben wasn't shot at the camp. I was there until a quarter to five. Unless the doctor's wrong, and the time of death was on the late side—"

"Almost certainly earlier is nearer right," Dr. Smalley said. "On the death certificate I'll indicate the time of death as approximately three to three-thirty."

"So Ben was shot, kept somewhere, and then transported to the camp and left for me to find," Peter said.

"Daylight saving," Quinlan said. "It stays light till nearly eight-thirty. What time did you get back to the camp and find him?"

"About nine-thirty. I called the barracks not more than five minutes after I walked into the camp and found him. The time should be on your telephone log."

"It is," Stadler said. "Nine thirty-four."

"So we look for people who were out and around in the village from two to three-thirty," Stadler said. "After that Gleason was in cold storage somewhere, till it was safe for them to move him."

"Locked in the trunk of somebody's car, shut away in someone's house," Quinlan said. "He wasn't missing then, so they could just sit on him."

"When I left Ben just after two o'clock," Peter said, "he didn't have any kind of a lead to anything, didn't know where to start looking for one. He was just going to circulate. No more than an hour or so later he must have known everything and it wasn't safe for the killer to let him live. It's right there, between two and three-thirty. In that span of time, Captain, he stumbled on something you and your men have been looking for for six months, ever since Dick Robbins was shot and killed."

"Not the same gun, not the same man," Stadler said.

"Five minutes ago Quinlan was pointing out that all you had was not the same gun," Peter said. "One man could own a collection. His words." He pushed back his chair and stood up. "I'm going to find Brad Smith and tell him we've narrowed down the time Ben Gleason could have been circulating. His gossipy old ladies could have been on their front porches in the early afternoon."

"I'm not sure I should let you go anywhere, Styles," Stadler said.

"Give me a man to go with me, then," Peter said. "Every hour that goes by, Captain, the chance of finding what Ben Gleason found grows slimmer."

“I'd like to tag along with Styles,” Sergeant Quinlan said, his voice deadly quiet. “The sonofabitch who killed Dick Robbins is out there close enough for us to touch!”

Mike Quinlan took time to stop at his locker in the barracks and change out of his uniform. In navy blue slacks, a plaid sports shirt, white buck shoes, and a corduroy jacket he looked more like the country-club set than a policeman. He and Peter decided to ride together in the Toyota.

“Even your friends back away from a uniform and a car with blinking lights on the roof,” Quinlan said. “Off duty I'm one of the boys! Cops are supposed to be your friends, but even innocent people tighten up when we're around. You're calling the shots, Styles. What comes first?”

“Brad Smith, if we can find him. It will help him to know the time span we've established. Judith Larsen wasn't very far away during that same time span; she may have seen Ben, even talked to him. Maybe you can make some kind of a dent in George Wilson that I can't. He's got to be persuaded that Judith's absence is important to us. He must know who friends of hers are to whom she may have gone. You and your wife have no idea?”

“A friend is a friend is a friend,” Quinlan said. “She went to school in this area. She knows a whole generation of kids. But after Dick was killed there seemed to be nobody close. I'll give Wilson a hard time for you.”

“Finally, I'd try to catch up with a young man named Bill Steele, who sails a boat just off the camp. The vandal or vandals who came to the camp and destroyed my stuff came there in daylight, yesterday—I guess it's day before yesterday now. Steele seems to be aware when I come and go. He may have noticed someone. I'm told I might find him at the country club.”

“I know Billy Steele quite well,” Quinlan said. “My age,

twenty-eight. Never had to lift a finger to make a buck in his life. Never will have to. Cyrus Steele's only child. He'll come into so many millions he won't be able to count 'em."

"Just waiting, out on the lake in a boat?"

"He keeps himself occupied—with women, drinks too much, caught with drugs in his car." Quinlan glanced at Peter, who was heading the Toyota toward the village. "One of the things about my job I don't like. I've picked Billy up several times DWI. Each time I took him home instead of pulling him in."

" 'DWI'?"

"Driving while intoxicated!" Quinlan said. "We have our orders. No accident, we handle the rich with kid gloves."

"You overlook drugs?"

"Not exactly. Dick Robbins caught him that time. Drunk, cocaine in the glove compartment of his car. Family lawyer promptly in the picture. Billy claimed he knew nothing about the coke. Someone who'd been riding with him must have slipped it in the glove compartment and forgotten it. Who'd been riding with him? List as long as your arm. Medical examination at the time indicated no drugs in Billy's system. He could have been telling the truth. If he was, someone on his long list of friends who'd ridden with him was lying. He got off."

"No drunk charges?"

Quinlan shrugged. "No accident. That's the way Stadler and the local justice of the peace play it. If it had been the local plumber's son they'd have thrown the book at him."

The *Advocate* office was lighted and a half a dozen young people were on the job, but not Brad Smith.

"Wherever Brad is he's not happy," a young girl told Peter. "Half a dozen big-city reporters following him around. No way for him to get done what he wants. People won't talk in front of strangers."

"Reporters looking for you, too, Mr. Styles," another girl said.

The little group was in shock over the dreadful news about Ben Gleason. They had all liked him, he had no enemies. Nobody in the office had seen him since early afternoon—now yesterday. He'd stopped by to get his car shortly after two o'clock, hadn't hinted where he might be going.

"It's like he was killed by a hit-and-run driver," one of the girls said. "No reason for it to happen. Just like a terribly unfortunate accident."

"He wasn't left beside the road," Quinlan said. "Someone hid his body for several hours and then carried it down to the Jordans' camp and left it there for Mr. Styles to find. Nothing accidental about that, Betty."

A kind of numbed silence followed that. Nothing so grotesque can happen to anyone you know and like, except it had happened.

"Did Ben have a girl, a special girl?" Peter asked. "He could have been in touch with her, told her something he never got to tell us."

The girls looked at each other like people who shared a secret. Finally the one named Betty answered. "I—I don't think there was anyone special."

"You know there was," Quinlan said. "Donna Littlejohn." He turned to Peter. "Everyone thought they'd hook up someday. One day she turned up married to another local boy, Jack Newsome. He's George Wilson's foreman, by the way."

"That's so long over," Betty said. "Ben never sees—saw—her, or had any contact with her. But he's never had a number-one girl after Donna."

On the way out to the car Peter commented to Quinlan, "Have you noticed that everything that touches this case has a connection with George Wilson? Judith's father worked for him, Judith's mother married him, Dick Robbins was about to become his son-in-law, Judith is his stepdaughter, now it turns out that Ben Gleason's girl friend married his foreman."

"Small town," Quinlan said. "George hires about a third of the work force in this town, all local. They all went to the same schools, intermarried, were related in the first place. Nothing freakish about a busy man in the community touching a lot of bases."

They drove on down toward the center of town.

"I never saw Wynwood like this," Quinlan said. "Going on one o'clock in the morning and the whole damn place seems to be up and around! Not a dark house anywhere. A crazy killer on the loose has really got 'em up-tight."

"Let's try Wilson next," Peter said. "I'd feel a lot less up-tight myself if I knew Judith was home or he'd had some word from her. If she heard the news late, on her car radio, she can have been trying to reach me at the camp."

"You can't be everywhere at once," Quinlan said. "Hello! Activity at Maxi-Service. You want to pull in for a minute? Wilson may be there."

The yard outside the barns and sheds of George Wilson's Maxi-Service was brightly illuminated by floodlights. There were several cars parked there and men circulating and talking together.

Peter pulled the Toyota up behind one of the parked cars. A youngish man in work clothes came over to his side of the car and peered in.

"Oh, you're Styles, aren't you?" the man said. "We got nothing here for the press, Mr. Styles." Then he looked past Peter and saw Quinlan. "Hey, Mike! Where's your soldier suit? You turned private eye?"

"We were just talking about you," Quinlan said. "This is Jack Newsome, Styles, the Maxi-Service foreman."

"I hope whoever was talking wasn't slandering me," Newsome said.

"Just happened to mention your name and I told Styles who you were. How's Donna?"

"Fine, if you can be fine when you're six months pregnant," Newsome said. "You really got something started here, Mr. Styles. Whole town is on its ear."

"I'm not exactly the one who started something," Peter said.

"Ben Gleason was working with you, wasn't he?"

"Yes."

"Too bad," Newsome said. "He wasn't a bad kid, though I had to kick ass on him a couple of times. He was sweet on Donna, my wife, before she married me. He seemed to think for a while he was still in the ball park."

"You see him at all yesterday, Jack?" Quinlan asked.

"If you mean to talk to, no. Like a lot of people in this town he was part of the landscape. Maybe I saw him around somewhere yesterday, maybe it was the day before. You don't put it in the computer. Incredible and I were on night patrol yesterday, midnight to eight in the morning. I was asleep after that till early afternoon."

" 'Incredible'?" Peter asked.

Newsome smiled. He had uneven, tobacco-stained teeth. "Howard Lomax is my partner on the night patrols," he said. "Big guy. We call him the Incredible Hulk."

"What's cooking here?" Quinlan asked. "Looks like a convention."

"The boss has called in everyone," Newsome said. "We're about to start patrolling all the places where we work."

"I didn't know there were any vacant houses just now," Quinlan said.

"Hell, it's not the ones who are away who are scared," Newsome said. "It's the ones who are here! Stadler doesn't have enough men to make everyone feel safe. We're going to be back and forth, in and out of the big estates the rest of the night."

Peter had noticed a bulge under Newsome's work jacket. "You all armed?" he asked.

"The bastard that killed Gleason isn't carrying a toothpick," Newsome said.

"How many men are involved in this special patrol?" Peter asked.

"We got twenty-eight of our own," Newsome said. "We usually ride double, but tonight twenty-eight cars are patrolling." He laughed. "One thing's for sure. No one's going to be prowling around this town tonight. Piece of advice for you, Mr. Styles. Go back to the camp and stay locked in there. You'll have both the troopers and our guys making sure you're safe there. When it gets to be daylight, things should get back to normal."

"Is Wilson here, directing things?" Quinlan asked.

"He's out around somewhere, checking all points," Newsome said.

"We're trying to locate Judith," Quinlan said. "You seen her around?"

"That little lady doesn't hang out down here with the common people," Newsome said.

"You sound as if you don't like her," Peter said.

"You can't not like somebody you don't know," Newsome said. "You know there's only one person in this town, rich or poor, high society or shit shoveler, who doesn't say hello when I pass them on the street? Even strangers say hello in a town like this. But not Miss Nose-in-the-air."

"I think she's just shy," Quinlan said.

"And had to take too much," Peter said.

Newsome laughed. "Could be, I suppose. Donna tries to tell me that. But, hell, her old man, Kurt, was my boss when I first came to work here. Great guy. We were friends. I used to drop in at their house and Rose would always have a cup of coffee for me and pass the time of day. The kid, Judith, wasn't around much, but she wasn't snotty when she was. Then Kurt's number came up. I wasn't married yet then, you understand, just one of Kurt's crew. The kid seemed to freeze toward everyone then. Then George and Rose got together, and since then Judith has been impossible. She drives by the yard here, looking like she smelled something bad!"

"But you haven't seen her in the last few hours?"

"Too busy to notice," Newsome said.

"We'll check up at the house," Quinlan said.

"Take my advice, Mr. Styles," Newsome said. "Go back to the camp and lock yourself in while this creep is still on the loose."

"If you're patrolling we'll probably see you around," Quinlan said.

"Don't jump out from behind a bush," Newsome said, grinning. "Everybody's real on edge tonight."

Peter turned the Toyota and headed up the rise toward George Wilson's house. Through the trees they could see the house, lighted upstairs and down. Even with George Wilson's army only a few yards away the ladies in the house were not running risks.

Drawn across the road at the top of the rise was a car. Peter's headlights revealed that there was no one behind the wheel. It was strategically placed so that there was no way around it except by running through an evergreen hedge.

"You lookin' for someone?" a voice came out of the darkness. It sounded like a young boy, Peter thought.

"Mike Quinlan, state trooper!" Quinlan called out.

A figure rose up from the floor of the car on the passenger side. It was a boy, armed with a shotgun.

"Gee, Mike, they told me down below anyone had any

business here would give me a horn signal." The boy got out of his car and came over to the Toyota. "Oh, hey, it's Mr. Styles, isn't it?"

Quinlan introduced the boy. "This is Freddie Thompson, Peter. He's a cousin of Ben Gleason's."

"When we got the news about Ben I wanted to help some way," the boy said. "Mr. Wilson wouldn't let me volunteer for the patrols. He thought the crazy man they're looking for might have it in for Ben's relatives. He let me stand guard here because there'd be help just down below and I have a CB radio in my car. I can reach Mr. Wilson in his car wherever he is—just in case."

"Did you see Ben anywhere, around in town yesterday afternoon, Freddie?" Quinlan asked.

"I haven't seen him to talk to for a week or so. Waved when we passed on the street." The boy gave Peter a shy smile. "That's my first car, Mr. Styles, a high school graduation present from my parents. I guess you can imagine I cruise around quite a little."

"And you knew who I was?" Peter asked.

"My older sister, Marlene, works at the *Advocate*," Freddie said. "I guess you could say we're a newspaper family. Mr. Smith has offered me some kind of job there in the pressroom after Labor Day. Marlene told us at supper last night about Ben finding your stuff ripped up at the Jordans' camp yesterday, and he joining up with you. Big deal for him, the way she told it."

"I'm afraid it cost him," Peter said. "Did your sister mention any thoughts Ben may have had about the case?"

"No, sir. Except maybe Judith Larsen isn't as crazy as we all thought she was." He glanced at Quinlan. "It must make you feel funny, Mike, to know that the guy who killed Dick Robbins is still floating around here in town. You and Dick were real close, weren't you? Same school and college. I got a picture in my room of the touchdown you scored against Pittsburgh. Dick was blocking for you. He's right in the picture with you."

"It feels funny," Quinlan said. There was a harsh edge to his voice. "But at least we know where to look now. We owe Mr. Styles for that. Is Judith up in the house now?"

"Gee, I don't think so, Mike," the Thompson boy said. "Mr. Wilson told me there was just Mrs. Wilson and Kay Logan, her nurse. He didn't mention Judith, and I can tell you she hasn't come this way since I've been posted here, which is about an hour."

"If she walked in there are a dozen ways she could come without you seeing her," Quinlan said. "I think we'll have a look. From all those lights, I imagine Kay Logan is still up."

Freddie looked uncomfortable. "I was told not to let anyone go up there, Mike."

Quinlan grinned at him. "You want to see my badge, Freddie?"

"Oh, gee, no! I'll move my car."

"We can walk up," Quinlan said. "Are you any good with that shotgun, Freddie?"

The boy beamed. "I won the trap-shooting prize in high school my senior year," he said.

"Then keep it pointed the other way when you hear us coming back," Quinlan said.

Peter and Quinlan walked up the road and across the lawn to the house. At the very first sound of the brass knocker on the front door a woman's voice called out from inside.

"Who is it?"

"Mike Quinlan and Peter Styles, Kay," Quinlan said. "Like to talk."

They heard a chain lock being disengaged and the sliding of a bolt. The door opened and the ample Miss Logan looked out at them.

"Saw you coming across the lawn," she said. "Couldn't

make out who it was." She reached out inside the door and produced a rifle. "Ready, just in case. Come on in." She glanced at Peter. "If you're here to ask about Judith again, Mr. Styles, no dice."

"No word from her?"

"Nothing. Look, come in, you two. Standing here in the doorway, in the light—someone want to take a shot at any of us—"

"Why would anyone want to do that?" Quinlan asked, as they stepped into the house.

"Mr. Styles may be a nice guy, but whatever he's got, it seems to be catching," Kay Logan said.

"Which is why I'm concerned about Judith," Peter said, not amused. "Wilson may have ordered you not to tell me anything, Miss Logan, but this isn't some kind of a quarrel between him and me. Judith, wherever she is, can be in real trouble. It's no longer a question of what you believe about her, or what she says happened to her, or that I am a stranger meddling in her affairs. We've got to find her!"

"Styles is right, Kay," Quinlan said.

"I don't have a decision to make, Mike," the woman said. "I don't have to decide whether to tell you something or not, because I don't know anything."

"Judith hasn't phoned? Wherever she is she must have heard the news about Ben Gleason by now," Peter said.

"Look, Mr. Styles, until about a half hour ago this phone has been going steadily. Mr. Wilson was here when the first call came about poor Ben. From what I heard it was Cyrus Steele calling. He broke the news and wanted protection. Mr. Wilson took the next calls down at the Maxi-Service shop. He told me, before he left, to lock up, stay inside, and stay off the phone. It would be busy. If Judith ever called, George got it down at the shop."

"You've lived in this house with Judith for how long?" Peter asked. "Three years, Miss Logan?"

"Give or take a month or two," the nurse said.

"She didn't give you the silent treatment, did she? After all, she'd need to ask you how her mother was doing."

"Oh, Judith and I have no war going," the nurse said. "But after all, there's a difference in our ages—and don't ask me how much!" She gave Peter an arch smile. "Let's just say I'm older than she is, didn't go to school with the same kids, no way I would have the same friends."

"It's her friends I'm interested in," Peter said, "because she may be with some one of them now, unaware of what's happened."

"You're thinking that three years under the same roof with someone would make them an open book," Kay Logan said. "That hasn't been true with Judith. I knew who she was when I first came here, of course. Used to see her in the village, sometimes on the street, sometimes in the coffee shop in the center. I remember thinking she must be a loner. She never seemed to be with other kids, not part of any gang, you might say. Then there was the accident to her mother and I was brought in on a permanent basis. Judith acted suspicious of me at first, but she watched me doing my job, bathing and dressing Rose, feeding her, putting her to bed for a nap or at night, wheeling her around in her chair. I guess she finally decided I knew what I was doing, and that I wasn't going to kick her mother around. That's when things got to be almost friendly. The main thing she was interested in was what I knew medically about her mother's condition, or what I could find out from the doctors. She was sure the doctors weren't telling her the whole truth. She had the idea that Rose knew what was going on around her but couldn't communicate with us. All I could tell her was I thought the doctors were leveling with her. Old Doc Smalley knows his business. 'Rose isn't ever going to know what's happening to her,' he told me. 'That doesn't mean you have a right to get careless, just because she can't complain about you.' " Kay Logan laughed. "At first if there'd been any reason to complain it would have come from Judith. She watched me like a hawk. Then, when she came to trust me, she began to get out and around. One New Year's she went to Fred Knowlton's party for the town. That's where she met Dick Robbins. She was a changed girl after that. She began to be able to joke and laugh. She would sit with Rose and tell her what a wonderful guy her guy was, even though Rose didn't know what the hell she was talking about. You could see she was suddenly concerned with how she looked. She had a little money left to her by her old man and she began to spend it on clothes. It sounds corny, but it was like watching a flower grow from a bud to a full bloom. And then bang! The end! Dick Robbins was dead, just the night before they were to be married. After that she was somebody I never knew before, a case for the doctors. No more conversations with me; almost as uncommunicative as Rose! Then the crazy story about a rape attempt that none of us believed. Then the second attempt, according to her, and you, Mr. Styles. Then the bullet, and now Ben Gleason! She could have been telling us the truth all along. You don't know where you're at!"

"Something I don't think anyone has told me," Peter said. "Who was supposed to attend the wedding in addition to you and your wife, Mike?"

"No one," Quinlan said.

"No other friends?"

"No. You see, she wouldn't have George Wilson present. Her mother couldn't attend. It would have made talk she didn't want if she had other people without asking George. She had to have witnesses, so she chose Nora and me. Period."

"And in all the time you've been under this roof with her, Miss Logan, Judith never mentioned any close girl friend?"

"She never talked to me about anyone except Dick Robbins after he came on the scene," Kay Logan said.

"Nor to Nora and me," Quinlan said. "We tried to persuade her to have friends present, but she told us there was no one who really mattered. I don't think she'd have had us if I hadn't been so close to Dick."

Kay Logan's smile was twisted. "She promised she'd save her bouquet for me—the one who gets the bride's bouquet is the next one married, you know."

"Then she liked you," Peter said.

"I thought so, at the time. But after Dick was killed she was a block of ice."

So much for a search for a friend of Judith's. Peter and Quinlan walked back across the lawn to the barricade Freddie Thompson had made with his car.

"Just keep aiming south, Freddie!" Quinlan called out as they approached.

They heard the boy laugh. He came out of the shrubbery beside his car, the shotgun held at the ready across his chest. He glanced up at the sky. "Startin' to clear up pretty good," he said. "Moon should light things up soon and I won't have to ask who's who."

Peter gave it one last try. "Did you go to school at the same time as Judith Larsen, Freddie?"

"I suppose you could say so," Freddie said. "But she was two, three years ahead of me."

"Do you remember who her friends were, the people she palled around with?"

"I didn't pay too much attention. When you're fifteen, sixteen, you don't pay too much attention to the girls eighteen or nineteen." Freddie grinned. "Maybe I should say it's the older girls who don't pay too much attention to the younger guys."

"But you noticed who she went with, who she hung out with?"

"Not really," Freddie said. "I mean, I guess she didn't go out with the guys we thought of as big shots at school. I mean, we were surprised when we heard she was going to marry Dick Robbins. He was the big hero type in town, big football star, real cool guy. There was a whole school full of girls we'd have thought he'd choose before Judith."

"She's a pretty girl," Peter said.

"And probably real nice if Dick Robbins wanted her," Freddie said. "She just doesn't let it hang out for everyone to see. Gee, Mike, I was sorry about Dick. And now all this! How can a town go sour all of a sudden the way we seem to have done?"

"One bad apple in the barrel," Quinlan said. "Keep an eye on the house up there, Freddie, and don't try to be a hero all by yourself. You see anyone prowling around call for help on your car radio. You just might wing the wrong guy. The town is full of strange reporters snooping around for a story."

Freddie grinned at Peter. "Like Mr. Styles," he said.

"I'm trying to help a girl who may be in big trouble, Freddie," Peter said. "The story comes later, after it's all over."

But where to look and how to help? Peter still had Billy Steele on his mind. There was a chance the young man might have seen someone snooping around the camp from his red sailboat out on the lake that afternoon—the vandal or vandals. Quinlan didn't think they'd find many people left at the country club.

"Most everyone is probably at home with their doors barricaded," he said.

He proved to be dead wrong about that. As they turned in the big stone gates, wrought-iron lamps lighting each post, Peter saw the brightly lighted old colonial building that was the clubhouse.

"One of the first rich men who settled in Wynwood gave his house to the town for a club when he died. It was a good start because he had a private golf course built around it. Damn good course, too. Wow, look at that!"

The parking areas around the clubhouse were crowded with cars. Far from being deserted, it seemed as if half the town must be congregated here.

"Council of war, I imagine," Quinlan said.

"Safety in numbers," Peter said. "Better to be all together than each one defending his own castle."

The only place they could find to leave the Toyota was about a hundred yards from the clubhouse. They'd only walked a few steps when a trooper stepped out from behind a car, hand resting on his holstered gun.

"Oh, it's you, Mike," the trooper said, relaxing.

"Trooper Collins," Quinlan said, introducing Peter. "What's going on here, Dave?"

"Cyrus Steele's running the show, I guess," Collins said. "He got all of his friends—and their friends—to come here. They're staying here until the troopers and George Wilson's boys have searched every estate and declared them safe. Seems like nobody wants to be alone, and we don't have enough men to post guards everywhere."

"Stadler goes for this?" Quinlan said.

"I guess so. He's in there with them. He and George Wilson are in there promising everyone they'll sweep the town clean in a couple of hours." Collins laughed. "The people are luckier than we are. Booze flowing in there like out of a tap. I'm supposed to keep anyone who isn't a member or a resident of Wynwood from going in there." He glanced at Peter. "Steele wants to keep the press out!"

"Peter's a resident," Quinlan said. "He has the Jordans' camp for the summer, and God knows he's part of what's going on."

"Yeah. So pass, friends," Collins said.

Collins was right. It was like a party in the clubhouse. Ordinarily, people would have been on the outside terraces in the summer moonlight. Tonight everyone was crowded inside, safe from a possibly crazy sniper. Men and women were jammed into a big dining room and bar.

There was laughter and a babel of voices. They weren't afraid here, apparently. On a little bandstand at the far end of the room, usually occupied by an orchestra for club dances Peter guessed, a kitchen-type table had been placed and Captain Stadler, George Wilson, and an older man, tanned brown with silver-white hair, sat behind him.

"Cyrus Steele," Quinlan said. "He's head of what they call a 'residents' committee.' I guess you could call him the unofficial mayor of the town!"

Someone took Peter's arm and pulled him away from Quinlan. He looked down into the bright, shining face of a young girl.

"A beautiful strange man!" the girl said. "Thank God, there's nothing here but the same old faces. I'm Sally Tabor. Has anyone bought you a drink, beautiful stranger?"

"I'm Peter Styles," he said.

"Not *the* Peter Styles! Oh, wow! Come to the bar, beautiful Peter Styles, and I'll buy you a drink. You can't buy because you aren't a member!"

"I have a guest card," Peter said. "I think that entitles me to buy. But—"

"But me no buts, my fine feathered friend!" the girl said. "Just remember, I found you first. There are a lot of other hungry females around here tonight. You've helped turn our town upside down, Peter. Just say your name is Jones when we step up to the bar, or I'm likely to be killed in the crush."

Peter turned to Quinlan. The trooper sergeant was headed for the table on the bandstand, obviously in response to a signal from Captain Stadler.

"Do you know Billy Steele?" Peter asked the girl.

She laughed. "Do I know Billy? Every girl in this town who hasn't got two heads knows Billy, want to or not! He's over there at the bar. He never gets far from the source of supply. I'll introduce you if you'll promise, afterward, to take me somewhere and tell me the story of your fascinating life. In return for that I'll show you my etchings! If you get what I mean! Follow me, lover. I'll run interference for you."

Billy Steele, close up, turned out to be a handsome blond man in his middle or late twenties. The sun on the lake had tanned him an even darker brown than his father. He smiled as he saw Sally Tabor, holding tightly to Peter's hand, almost dragging her captive toward him.

"Hello, Mr. Styles," he said, when they reached him.

"First, what are you drinking, Styles?" Sally asked. "Give the man what he wants, Juan." This to the red-coated bartender. "On me. And you can talk to him for just three minutes, Billy. He's mine!"

"I imagine it's open season for you, Mr. Styles," Billy said, grinning. "If you'll take a quick look around you'll see lust everywhere."

"After looking at you for the last ten years, Billy, can you blame us?" Sally asked. "A double vodka with a twist for me, Juan. I think my guest, looking at him, is probably a bourban man. If he won't tell you, try him on a Jack Daniels."

"I came here looking for you," Peter said to Billy Steele.

"Let me guess," Billy said. "Did I see anyone invading your camp yesterday when you'd left it—in the morning?"

"On the nose," Peter said.

"As a matter of fact I didn't," Billy said. "Stadler has already asked me. That was when they tore up your stuff?"

"Yes."

"Sorry, but I didn't see anyone."

"I've wondered why you always seem to be sailing your boat in sight of the camp," Peter said. "It's a big lake."

"You know anything about sailing?" Billy asked.

"Nothing."

"The lake is like a big football stadium, hills on three

sides, open at one end," young Steele said. "When there's no wind there's always something stirring at the open end, which is opposite your camp. Air seems to get sucked in there. When there's something really blowing you won't see me. I'll be all over the lake."

"But the last couple of days?"

"Almost becalmed," Billy said. "I've waved to you because I'm just sort of sitting there. I probably would have seen someone if they'd been open about getting into the camp yesterday. If I'd known what was going on then, you finding that bullet in the tree, I'd probably have come ashore. God knows there's been no excitement out there on the lake the last couple of days."

"It was a long shot, that you might have seen someone."

"Sorry," Billy said.

"Someone comes and goes like they owned the place," Peter said. "Key to the front door, apparently. First the vandalism, and then, after dark, they brought Ben Gleason's body there."

"After dark I'm not on the lake," Billy said.

"Three minutes are up," Sally Tabor said. "Here's your bourbon, beautiful stranger. Now for a cozy corner and another kind of violence—if you like!"

She had him by the hand again, tugging at him. He was saved by a loud voice, asking for attention. It was Cyrus Steele, pounding on the bandstand table with the bottom of a drink glass.

"Attention! May I have your attention, please!"

Peter turned and saw that Jack Newsome, George Wilson's foreman, had joined the three men at the table while he'd been involved with Billy Steele.

It took a moment or two for the laughter and talk to subside. Cyrus Steele had a deep, powerful voice. He was probably used to demanding attention. Board meetings, Peter thought.

"Jack Newsome has just reported that they've sighted the man we're after," Cyrus Steele informed the crowd.

Instant bedlam of voices again and Steele pounded on the table with his glass.

"This man," Steele went on when he'd gotten silence again, "wearing the ski mask that seems to be his symbol, was spotted just outside the Henry Kobler property. He ducked into the woods there when he was seen. Troopers and two of the Maxi-Service men are keeping the property under surveillance. We propose to go in there with as many troopers as can be spared, the Maxi-Service men, and as many volunteers as we can raise, and walk, shoulder to shoulder, through the Kobler property until we corner this monster."

"Or shoot him down!" Billy Steele shouted from the bar. "Count me in, Dad!"

The crowd broke into cheers and men began crowding forward toward the table. Apparently volunteers weren't going to be hard to come by.

"The whole world is going crazy!" A small voice said at Peter's side. He looked down at Sally Tabor. All the joy and fun had vanished from the girl's face and Peter suddenly felt cold fingers close on his wrist. "They've got enough guns here on the rifle range to equip an army. Now they've got a license to kill."

Cyrus Steele was pounding on the table again. "Quiet, please!" He was shouting. "I appreciate the willingness of some of the ladies to join us, but I think we must say no. But I urge all of you to stay here till we've done our job. The club will be guarded. It won't be safe for anyone to be wandering around carelessly till this is over."

There were comic moans of despair from the women in the crowd.

"There goes the Equal Rights Amendment," Sally said, a touch of her humor returning. "Tell me, Peter, why would this creep go wandering around town attracting attention to himself by wearing a ski mask? It's as though he wanted to get caught!"

"He's certainly drawn off most of the able-bodied men in town," Peter said. It was a question he'd been asking himself, and a possible answer presented itself. The man in the ski mask, spotted at the Kobler property, had accomplished exactly what he wanted. He had drawn troopers and Maxi-Service guards and a large portion of volunteer manpower to the Kobler property. When they started searching the woods for him all he had to do was discard his mask and join them! Meanwhile, what was happening somewhere else in town, unwatched, unguarded against? A red herring to cover what? A bank robbery? A kidnapping? The moving of another body—and Peter felt his muscles tensing—possibly that of a dead girl? Attention focused on the Kobler place, the real action somewhere else!

He looked over the heads of the crowd for Mike Quinlan, but the trooper sergeant seemed to have disappeared, sent somewhere on Stadler's orders, he supposed. Stadler himself was no longer at the table on the bandstand. Cyrus Steele and his son Billy were handling the enlistment of volunteers, and as each man signed on he hurried off. Outside Peter could hear the sound of dozens of car motors starting almost simultaneously. The men of Wynwood were taking the bait in a hurry—if Peter was right about it being bait.

"Where is the Kobler place?" he asked Sally Tabor.

"A couple of miles out of the center of town on Valley Road," the girl said. "You're not going, are you, Peter? It's not your war, is it?

"I wish I knew where the war was being fought," he said.

"Puzzle me no puzzles," the girl said. "Everybody's headed for Kobler's. They're not going fishing there."

"Or are they?" Peter said.

"I've had enough bewilderment for one night," Sally said. "I think of myself as a reasonably attractive, in fact irresistible, girl. Into my life comes a handsome stranger and I find I don't have what it takes. Couldn't we talk about that, Styles, instead of about all these silly jerks rushing off to hunt down a man who's playing Halloween games? Why don't I ring your bell, even a little bit?"

He looked down at her. "Because, my dear, very attractive Sally, my bell is diconnected for the moment. Yesterday afternoon a young man who was working with me was murdered, and later on his body was dumped on my living room rug—wearing a ski mask. The night before a girl came to me for help because she'd been attacked by a man—wearing a ski mask! Six weeks ago this same girl was raped by a man—wearing a ski mask. So maybe you can see why I don't think of what's going on as a Halloween prank. And perhaps you can understand why my 'bell' is disconnected."

"I'm sorry, Peter," the girl said, genuinely contrite. "The world is so full of horrors these days that you have to invent games in order to stay sane! What's happened to you you have to believe is real. I guess I know it is, but when I admit it I'm suddenly scared out of my wits."

"It's a time to be scared, but not for you I should think," Peter said. "You've had no connection with Ben Gleason or Judith Larsen, have you?"

"Poor old Ben. I had a sort of connection with him," Sally said.

"Oh?"

"A nice local boy," Sally said. "He was crazy for a friend of mine, Donna Littlejohn. We're a very snooty society here in Wynwood, Peter. Girls on my side of the tracks are not supposed to get interested in boys from the other side. We girls have a slightly different view of things. A man is a man. Ben was a pretty nice little hunk of man, and a lot of us envied Donna, who was making out with him in spades."

"An affair?"

"I guess that's the old-fashioned phrase for it," Sally said. "She was having sex with him and apparently loving it. Then one morning she turned up married to Jack Newsome, who is from way further on the other side of the tracks. I mean, maybe he can't even read or write."

"I met him earlier tonight," Peter said. "George Wilson's foreman at Maxi-Service?"

"That's our Jocko," Sally said. "Ben was like shot between the eyes." She lifted her hand to cover her mouth. "Oh dear, that's not the thing to say about him now, is it? I mean he was floored. He came to me, along with other friends of Donna's, to try to find out what had happened. I knew, but I couldn't tell Ben because I'd sworn to Donna that I wouldn't."

"What did happen?"

"I just told you, I swore I wouldn't tell. But—let's say, some people have different problems than others. In college Donna got hooked. Drugs. It was the style a couple of years back. She, you could say, got caught with her defenses down."

"But why Jack Newsome?"

"You can be had by anyone when you're off in a dream world," Sally said. A frown scarred her forehead. "I know. I traveled that road for a short while. I got lucky. I found out how to quit."

"So you couldn't tell Ben because you'd promised?"

Her smile twisted into a bitter downturn at the corners of her mouth. "I offered to cheer him up but—I didn't ring his bell either. I told myself that it wasn't because I didn't have what it takes, but because he was still far-out gone on Donna. I'll bet the poor guy was thinking about her at the last moment before someone shot him." She looked up at Peter. "I'm not as big a sex queen as I try to make myself out to be, Peter. But I could be and *will* be when the right stranger comes along." Her smile was back to normal. "You had me hoping there for a few minutes."

Peter looked around. As far as he could see he, the bartender, and three or four really old men were the only males left in the club lounge. He turned back to the girl.

"I'm going to run a risk with you, Sally," he said. "I'm going to tell you what I think and what I'm going to do about it. In case I should disappear, like Judith Larsen, or wind up in somebody's house with a ski mask over my head and a bullet in my brain, I'm going to ask you to call someone and tell them what I'm now going to tell you."

"Peter! You sound serious!"

"Dead serious," he said. He led her away, out of range of the red-coated bartender's hearing. "I think the man out at the Kobler place—the ski-masked gent—is a hoax. I think he's accomplished what he set out to do, draw the whole male population, plus the cops and professional watchmen, out there. I think some other kind of action is taking place somewhere in town, unobserved, unobstructed. Everyone in Wynwood who isn't here is out at the Kobler place or locked up in their houses. Lady Godiva could ride down the village green and no one would see her."

"What a fun idea!"

"There isn't much fun connected with it," Peter said. "Ben Gleason got wind of it, and he's dead. Judith Larsen got some kind of wind of it and she's missing, I hope not dead. If I've got my facts straight, six months ago Trooper Dick Robbins saw somebody drive out of the Kobler place, gave chase when the driver took off, forced him to stop, and was shot for his trouble. The Kobler thing may be a coincidence and it may not. Something is cooking here in town, and unless somebody looks for what it is, it's going to be pulled off, unmolested."

"But why don't you go to the troopers?"

"Because I don't know who to trust," Peter said.

"You're serious?"

"Dead serious." Peter took his wallet out of his pocket, extracted a card and wrote Frank Devery's name and unlisted number on it. "If I don't check with you by daylight—by breakfast time, Sally—call this man at this number. Tell him just what I've told you. He's my boss at the magazine. He'll know exactly what to do."

"Why don't you call him now?"

"Because whatever is happening is happening," Peter said. He smiled, bent down, and kissed the girl on her cheek. "If I've guessed wrong about you, Sally, I promise you I'll come back to haunt you."

"You haven't guessed wrong, beautiful stranger," she said.

He started to go and she walked along with him.

"Something—when you were talking to Billy Steele struck me," she said. "About the people who got into your house must have had a key. Di Summers is the agent for the camp, isn't she? Have you asked her?"

"Yes. She gave me the only key she had. Doesn't know of any other."

"She must not have been thinking," Sally said. "There's someone who has a key to almost every house on this side of the tracks. He takes care of the outside work at your camp."

"George Wilson?"

Sally laughed. "My father calls him 'the Keeper of the Keys.' He always says if George Wilson wasn't an honest man he could steal us all blind, having the key to everyone's house! But I guess he's honest because no one's been robbed."

Peter rested his hand on the girl's shoulder. "Say sweet nothings to me—if I come out of this in one piece," he said. "You might be surprised how loud my bell might sound."

2

Suspicion, Peter thought as he walked out into the parking area, is a crippler. Almost always, when he was on a story, there was some kind of danger when he began to see the light at the end of the tunnel. But almost always there was someone he could depend on for help—the police, someone on the staff at *Newsview*, a trusted friend in the area. Wynwood was something else again. There was no one he could feel sure of. Something about Captain Stadler turned him off. He had certainly been part of what, just possibly, had been an innocent conspiracy in the case of Judith Larsen. He; Sergeant Quinlan and his wife, Nora; Dr. Smalley and the psychiatrist, Dr. Kreuger; George Wilson—they had all been a part of a situation in which Judith had been catalogued as psychotic and a liar. Some of them could have genuinely believed the girl was sick, but somehow Peter couldn't shake the notion that one or more of them could have had a criminal reason for promoting the idea that she was sick. Which ones were in which category? The end result was that he felt he could turn to none of them for help. The one person in town he could be reasonably certain of was Devery's friend, Fred Knowlton. It was interesting that Knowlton hadn't been at the country club, following Cyrus Steele's lead.

What was going on in this strange town, split down the middle, dividing the rich residents from the locals? What could trigger rape, terrorizing a girl, destruction of Peter's property, and murder—two murders, because in Peter's mind the shooting of Trooper Dick Robbins with the same gun that was used to fire at Judith in her flight for help was a part of the total picture. The end result of this thinking was that he was alone. Even Brad Smith, the editor of the local paper, wasn't to be trusted totally. Smith had admitted to making things easier for George Wilson because of a substantial advertising contract.

Everywhere there was cover-up. Yet Ben Gleason must have discovered what it was all about in the space of an hour, in broad daylight, with people everywhere. Yet no one—unless Brad Smith's old ladies in their rocking chairs had reported something to the editor—no one seemed to have seen Ben Gleason, talked to him. Someone had to be covering up in spades.

Trooper Collins was still in the parking lot as Peter headed for the Toyota.

"Ladies in the clubhouse have to be protected," he explained to Peter. "You decided to join the others down at the Koblers'?"

Peter hesitated. "That's where the action seems to be," he said.

"You know where it is?" Collins asked.

"Valley Road, about two miles out of town, I was told."

"You won't be able to miss it," Collins said. "There'll be fifty or sixty cars parked along the main highway. Everybody and his uncle is headed that way."

Between two and three o'clock the afternoon before, Ben Gleason had been a man who had gone from knowing nothing about the case they were covering to knowing so much about it that he had to be silenced. At that point in time Ben Gleason hadn't been looking for Judith Larsen. She hadn't been missing then, or, at least, no one had thought of her as missing. The story Ben was working on as a reporter was the case of the man in the ski mask who had chased Judith off her property the night before, fired a shot at her as she tripped and fell in her attempt to escape to the Jordans' camp, using the same gun that had been used to kill Dick Robbins six months before. A second part of the story Ben was working on was the vandalism at the camp, the destruction of Peter's typewriter, his papers, his clothes.

At the time Peter had left Ben at the *Advocate* office, where his car was parked, the young reporter had had no idea where to head. He was just going to "keep my ear to the ground." In the space of an hour he had heard something, seen something, remembered something—a sound, a sight, a memory that had been fatal.

Peter drove his Toyota out onto the main highway through the country club gates. He drove slowly, trying to put together a puzzle for which too many pieces were missing. The careless use of the gun that had been used in a murder to frighten Judith was the starting point. The man in the ski mask night before last hadn't meant to kill Judith, just frighten her. She'd have been an easy target for him if he'd meant to do more than frighten her. The rape scene, six weeks ago, by the bigger man in the ski mask could have had the same motive—to frighten the girl, Peter thought. She hadn't actually been sexually assaulted, just mauled, pummeled, stripped naked. The object was to frighten her. So that what? So that she wouldn't go down to her property, the place where she and Dick Robbins had planned to build and live, at night? When she'd gone there again the night before last, she'd been frightened off again. Why?

Peter remembered, with a kind of grim humor, a line from one of Stephen Leacock's wonderfully comic stories. Leacock described his hero as "riding off in all directions at once." Where to start? Where to aim? The one place not to go, he told himself, was the Kobler property. That was where the enemy wanted him to go, wanted the whole town to go. That was *not* where the action was.

The town was strange. Twice on the way into the center a car went racing past him in the opposite direction, headed for the Koblers' he assumed. Everywhere along the way there were lights in the houses, but he didn't see a single person anywhere, not even a dog or a cat out on this warm, moonlit night.

There were still lights burning in the windows of the

Advocate's office. The chances were that Brad Smith, the editor, would have followed the leaders out to the Kobler property, but he was worth a try. The "old ladies in their rocking chairs" might just have come up with something.

Peter got out of his car and went to the door of the office. It was locked, but through the glass top Peter could see two of the young women on the staff sitting by the telephone switchboard. He knocked sharply on the glass. The inside picture was one of instant panic. The two girls clutched at each other, seemed to confer, and then, very tentatively, one of them came toward the door. The other was frantically dialing a number on the phone.

The girl who came to the door shielded her eyes from the light and peered out through the glass. Instantly she turned and called out something to the girl on the phone. Then she unlocked and opened the door.

"I'm sorry, Mr. Styles. We're still a little jumpy."

"I seem to have heard that other places tonight," Peter said. "Mr. Smith not here?"

"He's gone out to the Kobler place, with all the out-of-town reporters at his heels," the girl said.

"Did he ever say anything about getting on Ben Gleason's trail?"

The girl shook her head. "Only that nobody seems to have seen Ben after he left here."

"Sorry if I scared you," Peter said.

"What scares me more than you," the girl at the telephone said, "is that they have a secretary answering the phone at the barracks. All the troopers are out on patrol. They'll try to reach someone on a car radio if we really have trouble! That's like calling the fire department when the building has burned down!"

"But I guess they've got the killer cornered at the Kobler place," the girl at the door said. "You didn't go out there, Mr. Styles? That's where the story is, isn't it?"

"That's where it's meant to be," Peter said. "I'm more interested in Ben, what he did, where he went."

"I wish I could help," the girl said. "After all, he was our man."

Peter went back to his car, got in behind the wheel, and just sat there. Ben must have done just that, gone to his car, trying to think what his next move should be. What was on Ben's mind then must have been, exclusively, the vandalism at the camp. Judith, as far as he knew, was still being questioned by Captain Stadler up at the Wilson house. So he was thinking about the vandal or vandals. What had there been about the scene to grab at? Peter brought his fist down on the steering wheel. The vandals had a key! Ben would have known something that Peter had only just learned from Sally Tabor. Maxi-Service was "the Keeper of the Keys"! The keys must be kept in some regular place. There were dozens of houses in the care of George Wilson's men. Maxi-Service did outside work for the Jordans at the camp. Peter could imagine Ben Gleason asking himself where the key to the camp was kept, if one man carried it, if by any chance it was missing. Maxi-Service wasn't more than a quarter of a mile away, off the village green to the left. If Ben's thinking had been like that, Maxi-Service could have been his first stop after he left the *Advocate* office.

Maxi-Service, Peter thought, would be deserted now. Wilson's whole crew was out at the Kobler place or patrolling some of the other estates. But there might be someone there monitoring the phone. Freddie Thompson might still be up the hill guarding the road to Wilson's house. He might know something about the keys.

It was, at least, a move to make.

Peter drove along the green, took the left turn that led to Maxi-Service. When he had been there earlier with Quinlan, the yard had been brilliantly lit by floodlights. Now it was dark, except for the pale light supplied by the moon. Peter noticed several cars parked there. He was somewhat surprised. Jack Newsome had mentioned twenty-eight men using all their cars. Just as he was about to turn in he saw several men moving out of one of the sheds. They seemed to be carrying heavy boxes that they were loading into the parked cars.

A car traveling at high speed in the opposite direction, probably headed for the manhunt at the Kobler place, forced Peter to delay turning into the yard, and in that moment he made a decision. He let his car slide on past the turn into the Maxi-Service yard and around a little bend in the road about fifty yards past the entrance. There he pulled over to the side of the road, stopped, and turned off his ignition and lights.

There is something about a climate of suspicion; anything the least bit out of the ordinary sounds immediate alarms. Earlier on Peter had seen the Maxi-Service yard at work at night. He had seen the floodlights that turned night into day. What were men doing there loading cars without a single light showing? Surely it was to avoid attracting attention. And hadn't Newsome made it clear that all of Wilson's men were committed to patrol duty?

Peter got out of his car and cut back across a little rocky elbow of land toward the Maxi-Service yard. An isolated cottage off to the left, windows lighted, was the only sign of life. Higher up there was a glow of light in the sky that he guessed must come from the Wilson house, shielded from direct view by a clump of trees.

Over a little rocky ridge and down the other side the yards came into view, the cluster of buildings dark lumps in the moonlight. And there was movement, cars to building, and back again. Peter walked, bent low, using the same kind of evergreen hedge he'd seen up the rise where Freddie Thompson had been parked to hide his approach. He was only a few yards now from the first of the parked cars. He could see the license plate above the rear bumper of the car. It was a New Jersey car, not local, not Connecticut. He ducked down as he heard footsteps approaching. Two men were carrying a wooden box about the size of a child's coffin. They loaded it into the back of a station wagon just ahead of the New Jersey car. They spoke as they turned back toward the sheds. Peter couldn't hear what they said, but he was certain they were talking in a foreign language.

He edged a little bit closer to the station wagon. The men had left the rear hatch door open and he could see other boxes and cartons of different shapes and sizes. There didn't appear to be any labels, any names or addresses printed on the boxes. The license on the station wagon was from New York, not local, not Connecticut.

Glancing toward the sheds, Peter could see no lights there. The men loading the cars weren't risking a show of light of any kind. Peter wondered if he dared risk a dash across the open space to the buildings. Before he could decide his world came, momentarily, to an end.

A violent blow to the back of his head knocked him to his knees. Something like a bomb went off inside his skull. He was aware of a display of fireworks before his eyes and then—nothing.

Sudden throbbing pain as Peter opened his eyes—to darkness. He wondered for a moment if he'd been blinded, and then realized that he was lying in some totally dark place, away from the moonlight. He tried to move and found that his arms were securely tied behind his back, his legs held together at the ankles by some other kind of binding. Somewhere, some distance away—in another room Peter guessed—he could hear voices, muffled by a partition, involved in some kind of animated conversation. Again, something about the cadences suggested a foreign language, Spanish, Italian. And then there came a voice, loud enough to be quite clear.

"God damn it, we don't have any choice, do we?"

A jumble of voices in a jumble of languages.

Peter, very tentatively, tried moving. In spite of a blinding headache, he could turn his head from side to side without any difficulty. He seemed to be lying on something hard, like a wooden floor. He tried hunching himself to one side and took a tumbling fall, two or three feet he guessed, onto stone or concrete. The fall produced an involuntary cry from him. Instantly the voices in the next room rose. The argument seemed to increase, and was silenced again, this time by a quiet voice that had a familiar sound to it, though Peter couldn't place it.

There was the noise of a door opening, voices behind the opening louder, a thin sliver of moonlight, and then total darkness again as Peter heard the door closing.

"You were lying on a workbench," the quiet voice said. "You must have toppled yourself off. Are you all right?"

"Who are you? What is this?" Peter asked.

"A problem," the voice said. "Mainly, what to do about you, Peter."

"Do about me?"

"There are a number of alternatives," the voice said, "none of them particularly palatable."

"Palatable to whom?"

"Why, to us, my dear fellow," the voice said.

So familiar and yet Peter couldn't place it, couldn't put a face to the speaker.

"You see, we can't be sure how much you know," the voice said. "If you don't know anything we could just leave you here to be found in the morning by the Maxi-Service workers. But if you don't know anything, why did you come in here to spy on us?"

"An unfortunate curiosity about men working in the dark," Peter said.

"Unfortunate indeed," the voice said.

A cultivated, educated voice, familiar and yet it wouldn't fall into place for Peter.

"How much do you know about the work that was being done?" the voice asked. It wasn't really a question to Peter, but a speculation. The voice didn't expect an answer. "The reason it doesn't make sense to just leave you here is that when you are found, it will put an end to a very, very profitable venture. If you just disappear it may still be damaging to us. Who did you tell that you were coming here?"

"I'm not inclined to answer quesions," Peter said, "because I don't know what the result will be."

"Nor do I, my dear fellow," the voice said. "I don't have the authority to make a decision. The consensus out there is that we just put a bullet in you, cover your head with one of those grotesque ski masks, and drop you out in the woods somewhere."

"Wouldn't you leave me as a warning to someone, as you did Ben Gleason?" Peter asked, his voice harsh.

"There is no one left to warn," the voice said, "except a whole town." Peter could hear a deep breath being exhaled. "There is a possible solution in which I don't have much faith."

Peter was straining, in the darkness, at the bonds on his wrists. They didn't seem to give at all. The voice was coming to him from several feet away across the room. There was no way to get at the voice, and even if he could there were quite a few others on the other side of the closed door. He could hear the muttering of those voices.

"One thing I have learned over the years is that almost all people have a price. I wonder if you are that rare individual who can't be bought?"

"You have to have something to sell before you can put a price on it," Peter said.

"I suppose your salary at *Newsview* is about thirty-five, forty thousand dollars a year," the voice said, "plus expenses."

"You could have been working in the bookkeeping department," Peter said, and in that moment he knew, with a sense of shock, to whom the voice belonged. The man, invisible in the darkness, was Fred Knowlton, Devery's friend, a stockholder in the *Newsview* corporation. "Perhaps they send you an expense sheet with your stock dividends, Mr. Knowlton."

Again Peter heard that deep breath exhaled. "I suppose it was stupid to try to play games with you, Peter. I thought perhaps I could find out just what we're up against if you didn't know you were talking to someone you knew."

"What *you're* up against?" Peter said.

"Not just me, Peter, or it would be easy. There is a whole army of people. But you know that, don't you?" Knowlton's small laugh was bitter. "Everything runs so smoothly, so profitably, for so long. Then one thing goes wrong and it's like a dam breaking, like a landslide, like an avalanche. Three murders, an attempted murder, and now you, Peter. It was never meant to be like that. No one ever expected it to be like that. Tonight was supposed to be the end, at least for a while, and then here you are, snooping around in the middle of things. I don't think I can save you, Peter—because you're the kind of man you are."

"Do we ever come to the end of doubletalk?" Peter asked.

"Let me ask you a straight-out question," Knowlton said. "What would you take, in cold cash, to forget that you came here tonight, to forget that you saw strangers here, out-of-town cars, that you were attacked, trussed up, threatened? I'm not talking about a six-pack of beer, Peter. Say twenty-five, fifty thousand dollars?"

"In other words you're thinking of counting me in," Peter said.

"So far it's just a conversational ploy," Knowlton said. "Others will have to agree. God damn it, Peter, I don't want to be a party to one more death!"

"You were a party to others? You mentioned three murders and an attempted murder. You've lost me there. Two were your Dick Robbins and Ben Gleason. A third one and a try?"

"You haven't answered my question," Knowlton said. "Would you come in for fifty grand and—and a share in the profits for the future? It would involve one sellout. You'd have to write a phony story about the town of Wynwood and what you've seen and heard here. With your following, your prestige, you could turn attention away from us and earn your bonus."

"And have to shave tomorrow without looking in the mirror," Peter said.

"It would be better than dying, Peter," Knowlton said. "Three other men stumbled on the truth and they are dead. A woman who hit on it is a vegetable."

"Mrs. Wilson?"

"I'm afraid so. She was meant to die, but when she survived as a zero, she was allowed to live—if that is living."

"The three men?"

"Kurt Larsen. That wasn't an accident. He guessed what was going on, and he had to go. Dick Robbins, if he had seen the man in the car he stopped, searched the car, he would have known the truth. That had to be prevented."

"Not you! You cared for him!"

"Oh, God, no. Not me. Not me in any of the cases. But I am a partner. Yesterday there was young Ben Gleason. He came too close, snooping around, looking, he said, for a key to your house. He, too, came on the truth and that was that. Now, Peter, there is you. Maybe you know what's going on, maybe you don't. Either way the people out there don't believe you can be allowed to survive. If you know, you'll blow the game and a hundred people will go to jail. If you don't know, you're the kind of reporter who'll keep at it until you do. Too big a risk. I've been given the chance to persuade you to join with us, use your talents because you could use your public platform at *Newsview* to our advantage. You could be a rich man, Peter."

"If I say yes?"

"You'll have to persuade my friends in the next room that you mean it, aren't just trying to find a way to escape the moment."

"To manage that I need to know what I'm getting into," Peter said, in a flat, cold voice.

"Do you know what is in the boxes you saw being loaded into those cars outside tonight?" Knowlton asked.

"No."

"Probably two or three million dollars' worth of pure heroin, street value," Knowlton said. "My friends in the next room? Mobsters from all over the East Coast involved in the traffic. These aren't men who are playing for marbles. It's part of a huge business, probably bigger than anything else in the entire nation. Illegal drugs have made for a secret government more powerful than the old prohibition gangsters. Wynwood—peaceful, calm, gold-plated Wynwood—has become an important cog in a giant machine over the past few years."

"I don't understand."

"It happened through a kind of accident," Knowlton said. "One of the big shots—I suppose you'd call him a syndicate boss—came to Wynwood to visit Cyrus Steele. Cyrus is a man who has spent a lifetime trying to cheat the government out of taxes, make himself illegitimate profits. That makes him friends far outside the law. This syndicate boss happened to see the Maxi-Service setup here. One of his problems was getting drugs to the market past honest cops and federal men. This syndicate boss saw a way. Maxi-Service, with cars and trucks moving night and day, would be used. No one paid any attention to comings and goings.

Drugs could be brought here from Canada, from Mexico, from shipping points along the coast, stored here, and picked up and delivered by 'tourists' passing through. For it to work, George Wilson and some of his men had to be in on it. The payoff was too big for them to refuse. Cyrus Steele's support gave it a kind of legitimacy, and by now they are all getting too rich to be willing to blow it. There were so many ways to make it work. Wilson had access to houses whose owners were away. Drugs could be stored in a half dozen places at a time in town, so the action wasn't always here. I—well there are things you don't know about me, Peter—that Frank Devery doesn't know. Bad investments, something close to bankruptcy. Steele knew. He knows everything about everyone's finances. I could save my house, my life-style, by becoming one of them. I persuaded myself that dealing in drugs was no worse than dealing in liquor years ago, when it was against the law. What people want they will get, legal or not. And that's true, Peter. If you were allowed to smash this operation here, not one ounce of heroin would disappear from the streets. There would be a new setup, somewhere else. If you believed that and were willing to join us, you just might convince those men out there to let you live. Killing a famous reporter could keep the pot boiling far too long. If you can persuade them they just may take the chance."

"And if I can't, and they decide to kill me, you'd let them get away with it, Knowlton? But of course you would. You let them get away with murdering Dick Robbins, a man you really cared for!"

"I don't want to die, Peter," Knowlton said in a bitter voice. "If it's a choice between your living and my living, I choose me. We, neither one of us, will live, my friend, unless we choose to play along."

The door behind where Knowlton was suddenly opened. There was the sliver of moonlight again, the low muttering of voices, and then darkness. Peter was under the impression that more than one person had come into the room. The beam of a flashlight pointed across the room to a window. Someone crossed over and pulled down some kind of shade and a moment later Peter found himself blinking up into a fluorescent ceiling light. The room, he saw, was some kind of carpenter shop, tools in neat racks, the workbench from which he had fallen when he first regained consciousness.

Fred Knowlton, his face almost deathly pale, was leaning against a far wall, a hand raised to shield his eyes. He looked like a man who had just lost a war. Two of the newcomers were familiar to Peter: George Wilson, looking grim, and Jack Newsome, his foreman, smiling cheerfully down at Peter where he lay bound hand and foot. The third man was a stranger, dark skin, black hair, a neatly trimmed black moustache, wearing a well-tailored city suit. Dark eyes looked down at Peter as if he was some kind of nonhuman.

"Get him on his feet, Jack," Wilson said.

Newsome knelt beside Peter, grinning. "Don't try a dropkick, buster, or I'll let you have a good one." He worked on whatever was binding Peter at the ankles. "Hey, that's quite a plastic foot you got there!" He took Peter by the arm. "On your feet, chum!"

His legs felt numb as he reached an upright position, but Peter, arms still tied behind him, tried to stand steady.

George Wilson turned to Knowlton. "You put the proposition to him, Fred?"

Knowlton nodded. He looked as though he might be sick.

"You're not a man who takes advice, Styles," Wilson said. "You wouldn't stay away from Judith when I urged you and it's brought you to this. You wouldn't pay attention to warnings at the camp."

"Where is Judith?" Peter said.

"Finally got sensible and went somewhere," Wilson said.

"Am I supposed to believe that, knowing what I now know?" Peter asked. "You've known all along she was telling you the truth because you were in on what happened to her."

"She wasn't really harmed," Wilson said.

"Not like her father and mother," Peter said. "Not like her man."

"We just tried to scare her off," Newsome said. It obviously amused him. "Silly bitch began wandering around at night, back and forth from George's house to that property of hers. She was bound to notice the traffic down here. We wanted to stop her wandering. So first my partner, Howard Lomax, the Incredible Hulk, made like a sex maniac. Didn't do any good. She kept wandering. Couple of nights ago, when we knew a shipment was coming in, damned if she didn't start wandering again. So I scared her off."

"Taking a shot at her with the gun you used to kill Trooper Robbins," Peter said, very quietly.

"Robbins was unlucky," Newsome said, still smiling, like a man who was describing a party. "I was moving some stuff we had stored in the Kobler place. They were away. If Robbins had searched my car we'd had it."

"And did you fix the brakes on Kurt Larsen's truck and push Mrs. Wilson down her cellar stairs?"

Newsome's smile turned dangerous. "Nosy people usually get to pay for their nosiness. Maybe that goes for you, Styles."

"It goes for him," the dark man in the business suit said. "Whatever he says, he won't sell out. I know the type. Give him five minutes on the telephone and we're all through. I say let him have it, quick, and be done with it."

George Wilson looked steadily at Peter for a moment and turned away. "Take care of it, Jack," he said.

"You haven't even made him an offer!" Knowlton said.

"He'll agree, and turn us in," the dark man said. "That's the way it is, isn't it, Styles? Once a boy scout, always a boy scout." He nodded to Newsome. "Get it done."

Wilson, without looking at Peter again, turned and walked out of the room, followed by the dark man. From the pocket of his work jacket, Jack Newsome produced a gun that looked like a cannon to Peter.

"It won't hurt hardly at all, Styles," Newsome said.

"You don't suppose I can disappear without a search for the truth that will never end, do you, Newsome?" Peter asked, surprised at how normal his voice sounded.

"We'll run that risk," Newsome said.

"Someone will crack on you sooner or later," Peter said.

"Not as long as Domingo keeps the palms greased. Domingo's the big shot who just decided your future. He understands people. They don't want to die and they do want to get rich. He gives them an easy choice to make."

"He didn't give it to me," Peter said.

Newsome hefted his gun. "Any last words?"

Peter had been confronted by a psycho before. Newsome was looking forward to killing. There was no use trying to keep him talking, and yet . . .

"I've been trained to get answers to questions," he said. "I'd like to have a couple of answers before you pull that trigger. Are you responsible for Mrs. Wilson?"

"If you mean did I shove her? I went up to the house to talk to George. He was working at the books in his dining room. He thought his old lady had left the kitchen and gone upstairs. I talked business, and all of a sudden there she was in the doorway, eyes like saucers. She'd heard too much. Then she turned and ran and I knew she was headed for the phone to call the cops. I chased after her, gave her a shove as she was reaching for the phone. The phone was right next to the cellar door. It was unlatched, I guess. She just took a header."

"And Ben Gleason? Are you responsible for him?"

"Most of the dirty work seems to come my way," Newsome said. "He came here looking for keys. No one to ask, so he started looking by himself. He found the coke we're moving out tonight. He knew what it was. I just happened by and caught him. We thought maybe we could scare you off by planting him on you. But you don't scare, do you? So, I've run out of answers, Styles. You ready?"

They say when you're drowning your whole life goes before you. There wasn't going to be time for a single moment to be remembered. Newsome raised his gun in the classic style above his shoulder, and began to lower the barrel straight down at Peter's face.

There was a sound of smashing glass, a loud explosion, a scream from Newsome as his face seemed to dissolve in front of Peter. Peter dove for the floor and a corner of the room. He hadn't been aware of a skylight over this shop. A figure came down through the light, landing heavily just beside Newsome.

"You okay, Peter?"

It was Sergeant Mike Quinlan, still out of uniform. The door opposite him opened and George Wilson and Domingo, the dark man, ran in.

"One step further and you both get it," Quinlan said.

There is a kind of shock that takes over when you just miss a disaster—a potential car accident that is avoided at the last second, a fall off some high place that is averted by a last minute grab at something. An hour afterward Peter couldn't have told you exactly what happened in what he expected were going to be the last seconds of his life. Huddled on the floor, arms till tied behind him, he saw Wilson and the dark man called Domingo start to turn away in spite of Quinlan's warning, and there behind them was Captain Stadler and other troopers. He remembered seeing Fred Knowlton slumped down in a chair in the outer room, face covered by his hands, crying like a child. A trooper was standing by him, reading him some kind of warning.

Peter couldn't remember who untied the ropes holding his wrists, only the immense physical relief as he felt circulation starting up in his arms and hands. Then he was in a car with a trooper he didn't know, siren wailing. Minutes later he was in Dr. Jonathan Smalley's office. It wasn't until the old doctor began feeling around at the back of his head that he realized his headache had become almost intolerable.

"Probably a concussion," he heard the doctor say to the trooper. "Better get him to the hospital for an X-ray. Could be a fractured skull. God, what a blow someone hit him." The kind old eyes looked down at Peter. "Keep your fingers crossed, son. I think you may have gotten lucky, but we need to make sure." He held a hypodermic close to Peter's arm. "This should stop the pain, but it may make you real sleepy."

It wasn't until morning, daylight, that Peter woke and instantly wondered what he was doing in a hospital bed. And then it all flooded back. He hunched up on his elbow, felt no pain, and sat up in bed. Someone was standing by the window. It was Sally Tabor, the girl from the country club.

She came quickly to him. "Oh, Peter, you'll never forgive me, will you?"

"I don't understand," he said. "What are you doing here?"

"I didn't keep your secret," she said. "You were going where the real trouble was and not to the Kobler place. I couldn't keep it to myself, I was so scared for you. I went to Nora Quinlan, who's a friend, and told her. We went to the Kobler place and found Mike and told him." Her fingers felt cool against his cheek. "Will you ever trust me again?"

"You crazy girl," he said, "you saved my life!"

"You're going to be fine," she said. "Just a mild concussion Dr. Smalley said. Can you imagine, Cyrus Steele, Billy, Mr. Knowlton, and George Wilson, all in jail! Others, too. Peter dear, you really did a thing!"

"I blew it; you did it!" he said.

The door opened and Nora Quinlan came in.

"Alive and kicking, I see," she said. "Mike says to tell you he's sorry they cut it so fine, but that's the way it was. They looked all over for you, couldn't find you, and then spotted your car down the road from Maxi-Service. Captain Stadler and his troopers staked out the yard and Mike went on to the roof of the buildings, trying to find where something might be happening. And then he saw you, through the skylight, in the carpenter's shop."

"One thing that bothers me, Nora. There's not been a word of Judith Larsen. Those characters gave me a ton of information, but nothing about Judith."

"That's why I'm here," Nora said. "She's safe, she's fine."

"Thank God," Peter said. "But where—?"

"It seems that in the early afternoon, after Captain Stadler and Mike had left the Wilson house, she got a phone call. No one knew, no name mentioned. If she didn't get out of town at once, you'd be killed. You were her friend. She took off. She's just been wandering around the countryside in her car. The story has broken you know, Peter. Radio, television. She heard on her car radio that it was over, that you were safe. She couldn't reach you, so she called us. Mike says Fred Knowlton is blowing the whistle on everyone. He'll probably know who phoned her. I'm glad you look so well. I'm due at the clinic. I'll see you."

He leaned back against the pillows. The last tensions were slipping away.

"Peter?"

"Yes, Luv," Peter said to Sally.

"You never drank that Jack Daniels. When you're ready, I'll buy you another one."

He found he could laugh. "And I'll tell you the story of my fascinating life," he said. "Made more fascinating by you!"